SONGS
~ FOR THE ~
SHADOWS

SONGS
~ FOR THE ~
SHADOWS

CHERYL S. NTUMY

Atthis Arts

Songs for the Shadows

Cover Illustration by Akintoba Kalejaye
Cover Design & Cover Typography by Stephen Embleton

Edited by E.D.E. Bell

Published by Atthis Arts, LLC
Detroit, Michigan
atthisarts.com

ISBN 978-1-961654-16-7

Library of Congress Control Number: 2024942536

For anyone who has known despair.
You are not alone.

Foreword
by Wole Talabi

When we first began to create the shared world we now call the Sauútiverse in March 2022, our aim was to develop a creative sandbox that we and other African and African diaspora writers could play in for years to come. A shared world of imagination where we could use the settings, characters and concepts in a connected way, in conversation with each other, as a community.

We knew it had to be a world in which Afrocentric identities were the default, a world based on genuine African technologies, histories, philosophies, cultures, languages and worldviews, reimagined in a way that would allow us celebrate, interrogate and explore them in unique, beautiful and life-affirming ways. We knew it had to be a world that was rich, flexible, immersive and inclusive of different ways of being, abilities, sexualities and gender expressions—a world where all of the ideas from our diverse founding members could call home.

The result of our combined passions, skills and ideas was more vivid and thrilling than any of us could have imagined on our own. The Sauútiverse is a science-fantasy fictional universe, set in a five-planet system orbiting a binary star, where everything revolves around intricate magic and technological systems based on sound, oral traditions and music. United by a single creation myth, a creator goddess, an ancient founding civilization, and a root language of power, the varied aspects of the Sauútiverse are rich soil for storytelling. You can think of it like *Wakanda* by way of *Dune*.

Since the November 2023 publication of our inaugural anthology, *Mothersound*, which I edited, the Sauútiverse has grown into a thriving, ever-expanding fictional space with more histories, mythologies and socio-political dynamics being added and explored through story. Several Sauútiverse stories have been published, with many more to come, including novels, novellas and short stories. A follow-up anthology is in the works and more than a dozen Africans and members of the African diaspora are writing new stories in this world with us.

Songs for the Shadows is the first published Sauútiverse novella—a standalone in which we visit Órino-Rin, the planet where sound behaves in unusual ways, the echo planet Ekwukwe, known for its caves and terrifying fauna, and Zezépfeni, the binary star system's seat of power. It is a wonderful story about grief, but perhaps, more importantly, about redemption. The settings may be new, but the themes are universal. I fell in love with this story the first time I read it, I have no doubt you will too. I hope you enjoy this visit to the Sauútiverse and that you will visit again.

Wole Talabi

SONGS
FOR THE
SHADOWS

The Sauútiverse

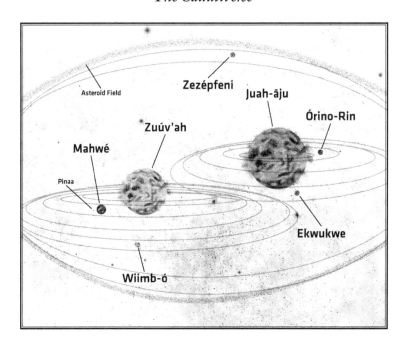

Asteroid Field

Zezépfeni

Juah-āju

Órino-Rin

Zuúv'ah

Mahwé

Pinaa

Ekwukwe

Wiimb-ó

1.

WHEN YOU could afford to host a syhh'ra in Ducha'ga, you knew you'd made it.

Yet Shad-Dari could only think of leaving. She stood with her shoulder pressed against the wall, nursing a cup of tesh'ii as she scanned the room around her, trying to distract from the sounds inside her.

Paint-adorned bodies lounging in the Tanti'ti shack, a bulbous tent of lightweight metal, floating far above the planet's surface. The gentle thrum of music muted to prevent cataclysmic clashes with ambient sounds. Guests breathing deep, knowing it was safe to do so up here in the clouds.

Traditionally, syhh'ra were intended as spiritual gatherings for Ts'jenene raevaagi, a chance for the nomadic historians to swap and store sonic stories away from the dense, soul-sloughing air of the surface. Now, the gatherings served a far more secular purpose.

Drink flowing till the floor was sticky with it. Hushed exchanges made under tables, a handful of owo for some illicit noise to take the edge off. The faint tang of desperation in the air, as though despite their privilege the partygoers were running from something too sure of itself to give chase. Something that waited for them, knowing its time would come.

Even though Shad-Dari had succumbed to social pressure and dressed the part in a purple abaya, collar and sleeves embroidered in silver, swirling henna designs on her fingers, it all felt so . . . predictable.

You've been here before. Remember?

The thought faded before Shad-Dari could process it, and then it was as though it had never come. All she could think of now was places she'd rather be.

Her crew, on the other hand, were having the time of their lives, enjoying the respite before another long dig in the morning. Fresh from a hero's welcome on Zezépfeni after what had turned out to be the most important dig of their careers, Fa'fali and Kga'arah lay on a pile of cushions surrounded by admirers, Fa'fali bragging in Sign: *Did I mention that the sound fragments we excavated were the oldest on record? Made by the First Ones themselves . . . We got commendations from the Council, even from the SeKarah of the Susu Nunyaa . . . Did I tell you it was my idea to pick that site? What can I say? The ear of the Mother guided me . . .*

Shad-Dari tried to focus on the music and laughter, but she could still hear that *other* thing. That whisper which never seemed to fade. That piece of home that had trailed her across the skies, an unwelcome shadow.

Sha-sha-sha-dar-dar . . .

Her echo. And all the phantom echoes that came with it. A face flashed into her thoughts, an old woman—both familiar and foreign, with eyes so deep they made her head hurt. She'd locked gazes with the woman, an outcast on the Zezelam beach, just as the excavation crew left Zezépfeni. Not a word had passed between them, but Shad-Dari had felt off-kilter ever since. As if the old woman knew something about her. As if she saw right through her.

Sha-sha-sha-dar-dar . . .

The echo was getting louder. Hungrier. She thought of the steps carved into the mountain, leading to freedom. Taking a long sip of her drink, she backed towards the door, glancing at her crew to make sure they were still occupied.

Rori'iro and Bed-Shek sat closest to her exit. The only Aq'pa on the crew, Bed-Shek's scales gleamed in the artificial light as she used her bare shoulders to shield Rori'iro's fake kartel tattoo from the very real kartel scions lurking near the window. Shad-Dari had to admire the boy's gall—for a teenager from Ekwukwe the illicit tattoo might be a fashion statement, but for the kartels it was a mark of belonging, something to be earned, not bought off shady vendors in the seedier parts of town. It might just ruin the party if Rori got himself thrashed for theft.

As Shad-Dari reached the door, Bed-Shek's gaze shifted to meet hers.

The Aq'pa cocked her head. *Sneaking out of your own party?* she signed.

Things to do, Shad-Dari signed back.

What do I tell the others?

Tell them if they break anything, it comes out of their wages.

Shad-Dari drained her cup, set it on the floor and slipped out. As the door closed behind her she exhaled, making her way along the rope bridge that connected the shack to the city of Ducha'ga, which was built right into the side of the mountain.

She grabbed one of several sets of breathing masks hooked into the bridge and put it on as she hurried through the darkness, holding onto the rope, fierce wind whipping her abaya around her legs.

Other Tanti'ti shacks floated nearby, some hooked to the mountain by rope bridges like hers, others simply hovering. She had bought hers from a Ts'jenene merchant who had fallen on hard times. Not because she needed it—Sauú3 provided accommodation for employees—but because she got a kick out of showing Ducha'ga groupies a good time. She'd loved the way their eyes lit up when they stood at the window of the shack, seeing their world from above for the first time. She'd revelled in their gushing gratitude, their starry-eyed adulation. *More.* That was all she had wanted then. Life, but faster, bigger. Up, up, up. And now all of it stifled her—the dizzying heights, the generous bonuses, even the recent commendation from the High Council—none of it enough to keep the demons at bay.

Reaching the rocky ledge at the end of the swaying bridge, her hands slid off the rope and over the metal hooks in the pillars on either side of the narrow path. The shack docking post was hers for the night, for a nominal fee. Come morning she would pull up the rope bridge and ground the shack until the next syhh'ra. Come morning, she could dispense with the pretense. Come morning, there would be silence.

She glanced down the narrow streets of upper Ducha'ga, where many of the top-tier sound excavators lived, and then took the winding steps to the lower levels. Down, down, down. She spared a thought for her abaya—a wispy, delicate thing her ex-girlfriend Essi'se had given her, back when Shad-Dari had thought she had it in her to be delicate. By the time she made it back from the meridian, the garment would be ruined. She wondered, for a moment, whether that was why she had chosen to wear it. After all, killing the memories was easier if the objects tied to them died first.

She increased her pace, the air growing denser as she descended, each step requiring greater effort. Even before she reached the edge of the meridian, she started to feel the unique sensation of reduction, of being kneaded and flattened like dough, flecks of her very essence flaking away in the vicious atmosphere. *Take it,* she told the planet. *Take it all.*

But she knew Órino-Rin's hunger was the patient kind, the kind that nibbled, never gorged.

Shad-Dari moved as quickly as she could through the streets, wary of pickpockets on the prowl for easy prey. She ducked into one side road, then another. Down more steps, into the belly of the port city, emerging into a murky market dense with fog, the air reeking of damp and rot even through her mask.

She found the entrance she sought—a rusted metal curtain in lieu of a door—and went inside without announcing herself. The crushing pressure of the outside world ceased instantly, blocked by a protective magic veil. The interior was dark, but she heard the uroh-ogi, the healer, scrabbling on the ground.

"Greetings, Mah Mmi'ino."

"Shad-Dari," the uroh-ogi said, after taking a moment to place the voice. "I wondered when I would hear of you again. How long has it been?"

A few scratching sounds and a flame appeared, then danced

its way to the wick of a fat candle. Like all who spent their lives on the meridian, Mah Mmi'ino's sound aura was a fractured shadow of what it had once been. Only the gifted could see or sense sound auras, but damage this extensive left physical traces, too. The woman was barely middle-aged, yet the lines in her face ran deep and her mind was cracking along with them.

"I was here only a few weeks ago," Shad-Dari reminded her, dropping to her knees on the faded rug that covered the floor.

"Oh?" The healer frowned, struggling to recall, and then nodded. "Yes, yes. Before the last storm." She added, with an edge to her voice: "So you've come for more mutilation."

Shad-Dari smiled at the dramatic word. "To heal a heart, sometimes you must break a finger."

Mah Mmi'ino kissed her teeth. "Quoting proverbs is not wisdom." She reached into a shadowy corner of the room and pulled out a large glowing crystal, which she placed on the rug before her. "What we do here . . . It harms you."

"I know." Shad-Dari produced a leather pouch heavy with owo and dropped it on the rug.

The older woman hesitated, as if she might refuse. After a moment she whispered, "Sit down."

Shad-Dari sat cross-legged on the floor and withdrew two tiny storage drums from her pocket, each the size of a fingernail.

Mah Mmi'ino clicked her tongue. "How long do you think you can steal from Sauú3 before they finally catch you?"

"Many juzu, apparently." It was hard to stifle the sense of triumph she felt as she said it. Was it her fault her dwandenki employers were so easy to rob? Besides, she only ever took slivers of sound fragments too small to be missed, a fraction of a second of a song, a syllable of a drawn-out word. The disruptions she caused were so inconsequential that no one would ever notice.

"Listen to you, so shameless!" Mah Mmi'ino's eyes grew wide in the candlelight. "Please tell me those are not from the latest dig. Not the sacred songs of the Great Seeding . . ."

A flash of irritation streaked through Shad-Dari's chest. It was remarkable how quickly news travelled on this planet. "Does it matter?"

The Susu Nunyaa order of spiritual scholars received all fragments to their temple on Zezépfeni and deciphered them for the rest of the planets. It was they who had confirmed that the sound fragments her team had found dated back to the Seeding—the arrival of the First Ones. The birth of humanity. Many on Órino-Rin resented Zezépfeni's monopoly over fragments not their own, while others believed that only Zezépfeni had the skill to manage the fragile artefacts.

Shad-Dari didn't care either way. She had thought Mah Mmi'ino felt the same. Clearly, she'd been mistaken.

"Yes, it matters!" The uroh-ogi kissed her teeth impatiently. "Stealing from Sauú3 or the Susu Nunyaa is fair. But stealing from the First Ones, from our ancestors . . ." She shuddered in superstitious fear. "Even you must have limits."

Shad-Dari spoke without thinking, words she had heard uttered a thousand times. "Like everything else Órino-Rin yields, the fragments belong to the people. It's not theft. It's reclamation."

"Nonsense." Mah Mmi'ino reached for the little drums and placed them inside the shells of Shad-Dari's ears with slow, reverent movements. "You are no radical. You just don't care about consequences."

The uroh-ogi was wrong. Shad-Dari longed for consequences. They were the ones that played coy, dodging her for reasons she failed to grasp.

"Begin," the healer said.

Her shoulders dropping with relief, Shad-Dari murmured an incantation, drawing energy from the glowing crystal on the floor, taking it into her body. Excavators were forbidden to use their own Mother-given sound in their work, for fear that it would taint the precious, delicate fragments they unearthed from sites across the five planets. Instead, they were trained in manipulating raw sound energy to do their bidding. While others reverted to their natural magic outside of work, Shad-Dari had abandoned her innate echo magic and made the Sauú3 techniques her own.

Wielding that raw energy like a brush, she raised her hands and made delicate strokes against the drums with both index fingers, loosening the rubber stoppers that kept the fragments in. She drew out only two of the four contained sounds—a cut-off, woeful cry and part of a whispered word—cloaked them in magic and then tightened the stoppers once more. Before the sounds could swell and fill the air, affecting Mah Mmi'ino, Shad-Dari guided them inwards, deep into her ears.

Her head pounded as she guided the fragments into her brain. Sacred sounds—especially sounds this old, this potent—were never intended to be heard this way. A memory of a memory, absorbed from the inside out, vibrations threading through the marrow before reaching the skin. Her breathing grew laboured. She pulled the fragments down to her heart and when she settled them in her diaphragm a wave of nausea struck, forcing her to swallow hard.

"Ready." She lay down, careful not to dislodge the drums stoppering her ears, and closed her eyes to let the uroh-ogi take over.

Over the time they had known each other, Shad-Dari had coaxed Mah Mmi'ino into forgoing her precise healing technique for a scattershot sonic assault. She prepared for the reactions, as the healer poured strong sound medicine into Shad-Dari's perfectly healthy body. The sensation was juicy at first, a delicious discomfort. Tingling in the bones, a vibration against the eardrums, as though Shad-Dari were made of music, a cosmic melody come alive.

The combination of medicine and stolen fragments was always unpredictable. This time, it made Shad-Dari's stomach turn. Pain lanced through her belly as if she'd drank poison.

Yet she could still hear her echo.

"Harder," she murmured.

The uroh-ogi tutted in protest. "Your echo is faint. I can barely sense it."

"I hear it like a drum." Pounding, pounding. Mother, why did it feel worse than usual? Her skull was full of throbbing noise, death throes and phantom whispers.

"It's only in your head, Shad-Dari." The uroh-ogi said this often, as though repetition would make it true.

"I don't care where it is. I want it gone!"

"Your tolerance is growing," Mah Mmi'ino said. "It will end badly for you."

Well, that was a given. When had it ever ended well for anyone? It didn't matter *how* it ended, as long as it did. That was all Shad-Dari sought. Peace. She gritted her teeth against the onslaught. Mother God, was that her sister's voice, creeping out from the folds of her echo? Why? Why couldn't the dead stay silent?

Opening her eyes, she grabbed the uroh-ogi by the front of her tattered clothes. "In the name of the Mother, just do what I ask!"

With a fearful nod, Mah Mmi'ino increased the pressure of her fingers against Shad-Dari's temple, tapping, pushing, moving down her neck and then slamming the heel of her palm into her chest. Once. Twice. Again and again, the burst of power intensifying.

Discomfort gave way to agony as magic flooded Shad-Dari's body. Every cell came alive with sound. Her body shook. She cried out, equal parts torment and relief as traces of her echo dissipated, vanquished at last.

For now.

Shad-Dari made her way from the bridge to the cargo bay of the *Nuseh-Tor*. Mah Mmi'ino's power still pulsed inside her, making her body thrum with pain.

She had not slept here on the ship, as was typical after a visit to the uroh-ogi. Instead she had slept on the other side of the city in her now-grounded shack, among the detritus of the syhh'ra. Never a good idea—even less so when she had a job in the morning—but traces of her former lover still lingered on the ship and Shad-Dari hadn't gone through all the bother of quieting one set of ghosts only to contend with another. She made a mental note to dispose of the rest of Essi'se's belongings at the earliest opportunity.

The door opened at the sound of her voice, sliding back to admit her into the cargo bay. Inside stood a tank filled with water from the Zezépfeni sea, pitch black in the dimly-lit space. The only sign of the seven creatures within came from the occasional pulses of light they emitted through their tentacles. The Mahu Mahadii had no equivalent for human conventions such as greeting and enquiring after the health of others, so Shad-Dari didn't bother.

"I'm sorry for the delay," she said. "We'll be taking off any moment from now."

Their reply came in vibrations rippling through the water. They spoke the way they did everything else—as a collective consciousness. It had taken Shad-Dari months to learn to decipher the vibrations, and several more to accept that they lacked the nuances of humanoid language. No poetry, no metaphor.

"Time is of no consequence," they said.

Like some ethereal cousin of Órino-Rin's swirling fog, the Mahu Mahadii's bodies were grey-blue clouds atop hundreds of tentacles. In the water they looked like tendrils of smoke curling around an electric current.

"The excavation site for today's dig is a lake in a sisu'um, a place dotted with small pockets of silence," Shad-Dari told them. "None of us know the place, but we're told it will be challenging. We'll set up in the sound patches and try not to move. It should be easier for you—the bosses believe that none of the silences extend below the surface of the water. Have any of you worked in a sisu'um before?"

"Those here have not, but we know how to navigate the silences."

"Good. Then we should be fine."

Shad-Dari didn't approach the tank. Something about the creatures always made her nervous, as though they could see her in ways her own species couldn't. Her fingers slid into the left pocket of her worksuit, where she had put the drums containing the leftovers of the stolen sounds she had used the night before. What would happen if she released them into the tank? Would the world end? Would the Mahu Mahadii even notice?

Silencing the wicked voice prompting her to take the risk, she asked, "Is it true that you can see the future?"

"The future doesn't exist."

She refrained from rolling her eyes. "Possible futures, then. How the dig might go. Where I might be a juzu from now." Whether the ghost echoes would ever leave her for good.

"Your fate is of no consequence."

"It's of great consequence to *me*."

They said nothing, floating there in superior silence. She couldn't tell whether they had no answer or had simply grown bored with the conversation.

"Do you know anything about . . . eh . . . ghost echoes?" Her tongue stretched out to moisten suddenly dry lips. "I mean the echoes of the departed. Echoes that linger."

"What is gone is gone. What remains, remains."

"That's not helpful."

They fell silent again. Staring into smoke and crackling electricity felt distinctly one-sided, even as she sensed them probing her with their otherness. Yet, she thought, if they had eyes she might feel less at sea.

"Let me put it this way," she said. "I know you have no interest in human notions of the divine, but you can perceive things of the spirit, can't you? Things that transcend time and space?"

There was a pause before they responded. "If one pays enough attention, one perceives all."

Shad-Dari stepped back with a weary sigh. Why did she keep trying? These beings had no interest in connecting with humans. "It must be liberating to care for nothing but your sacred sea," she murmured. "How I envy you."

"Your feelings are of—"

"No consequence. I know." She left the cargo bay, dissatisfaction heavy in her gut.

The Mahu Mahadii had no propensity for guile. Even though she knew their worldview differed from hers, she couldn't shake the conviction that they were right. Not just factually, but on some deeper cosmic level. If they said her fate didn't matter, it didn't matter.

Her fingers caressed the drums in her pocket, seeking an elusive solace.

2.

SOME NAMES were not meant to be spoken.

In many places all names carried vulnerability. People kept their true names hidden away, like drums of sacred sound. But in the caves of Tifaritu, on the planet Ekwukwe, names carried a person's essence and to speak them was a mark of respect. The Tifariti did not fear the names of their own.

Growing up in the unyielding echoes, born in darkness shielded from the sky, they knew the difference. Ravenous otherworldly beings that could not be seen, or worse, could not be heard—to utter *their* names was to summon them, and once they came they swallowed you whole, echo and all, and no trace of you would ever be found.

Those names you never spoke.

The stand-in for such monsters, such names, was Tlalala, a word that embodied an insatiable appetite, for it echoed forever. One could begin it and never cease, tongue locked in an endless dance—Tlalalalalalalalalalalalalala—until the end of time.

Tifariti children would hide deep in the network of caves they called home and dare each other to say it, testing how long they could draw it out before their breath gave out or their heads spun, or an adult overheard and came running to silence them. Even the stand-in name was dangerous, the elders said. A slippery slope. Not something to be toyed with.

Despite the warnings, or maybe because of them, Sha'dar'dar Se'seruwa toyed with the name daily, turning it over and over in her mind, trying to catch a glimpse of the true name it represented, or even the creature the true name signified. Sometimes, when she looked out of the corner of her eyes just so, she could swear she saw something on the periphery of her vision, some shift in the air. She could almost hear the faintest strains of a call on the wind.

She was not afraid of hunger. Sometimes she felt as though she were made of it, as though it laced the very air she took in. The second youngest of twelve children, with seventeen cousins, Sha'dar'dar was lost in a sea of dusty bodies and gaping mouths. She found the caves loud and oppressive—the crevices the children squeezed into at night, the hollows the adults claimed for sleep and storage, the huge cavern where the whole community gathered for market day, meetings and celebrations. She woke early each day to escape them.

Up, up, up. The sky and open air beckoned, along with the countless stars that seemed to sing her name. She would run through the network of caves, crawling through tunnels, fleeing past the spring near the marketplace, ducking neighbours as they emerged from their hollows, climbing up the rocks until she emerged at the top of the hill. She would scurry round to the other side of the hill and shout "Tlalala" with all the force of her echo behind her, daring the monsters to reveal themselves so she could witness *something*, something epic and important at last, something beyond the world of dust and noise and stone and half-full bellies. They never emerged. The name would die, snatched up by the wind, drowned out by the calls of wild beasts and echoes bigger and stronger than Sha'dar'dar's.

She was never home, if she could help it. Not when there were chores to be done, or decisions to be made, or rare feasts to be shared. So, at the age of fourteen, she wasn't home when a gang of amateur sound miners accidentally brought down three caves, crushing two families, including hers, to death. It was almost dusk when she returned from gallivanting to find a crowd still clearing away the rubble.

One of her aunts and three of her cousins survived, calling her to them from the bloodied blankets wrapped around them, through the crowd of wailing onlookers.

"She lives! Thank the Mother!" And they smothered her with relief.

Instead of comfort, they brought her pain. It was as though their echoes had swollen to contain the echoes of all those they had lost and the world had become louder than ever. A world of scurrying footsteps where there were no feet and whispers where there were no mouths. A new cave, smaller than the crevice she crept into each night. Sha'dar'dar couldn't breathe, let alone grieve.

Up, up, up! The call blossomed into a wild and desperate thing, fighting to be heard over the clamor of phantom echoes, until she could no longer bear it. So, she left.

※

"I have to go out."

Im'mii moved around the small room that had housed he and Sha'dar'dar for several weeks, picking things up, discarding them, and then changing his mind and pocketing them after all. His eyes narrowed at Sha'dar'dar, but her hands were safely in her lap, empty. She blinked innocent eyes at him.

"Will you be long, uncle?"

"No. Don't sit so close to the merchandise," he said, shooing her away from the wooden chest where he kept his best wares.

Sha'dar'dar scooted over, rolling her eyes at his theatrics. She had met Im'mii on a desert boat travelling from Tifaritu to H'ghale, one of the big Ekwukwe cities. A fence who specialized in stolen sounds, he had spotted the runaway and seen an opportunity, offering her room and board in exchange for bringing him new customers. She looked, he said, like the type who could convince someone to make a reckless decision. She still wasn't sure whether it was a compliment.

"Behave yourself," he said, "or I'll make you regret it."

"Yes, uncle."

Satisfied that his threat had done the job, Im'mii left.

"Never touch the merchandise," he had told her repeatedly. "You are young still; it will addle your echo. You hear?"

The warning was, in her mind, reason enough to disobey. But she had a more pressing reason, too. The ghost echoes had followed her from Tifaritu and not even the droning chants of the Susu Nunyaa from the nearby Zezépfeni-owned spaceport would quiet them.

Sha'dar'dar crept towards the chest and reached into her pocket for the key she had stolen earlier that day from under

Im'mii's mattress. The chest was filled with storage drums small as thimbles and a smattering of crystal shards. Ignoring the shards, Sha'dar'dar picked out one of the tiny drums and uttered the incantation to open it. She had been practicing, spying on Im'mii when he worked. It took a few attempts, but at last the drum opened with a pop, releasing the spell within.

Sha'dar'dar didn't quite understand the combination of alluring melody and poetic lyrics in the lost high Sauúti tongue, words she struggled to translate. Yet the ritual song made her knees buckle and her mouth run dry, and a sort of crescendo built inside her, exploding into a riot of noise and colour.

It felt good, so good, better than anything had to the right to feel. As she lay on the ground savouring the sensations, she realized that the echoes had gone quiet, as though cowed by the power of the spell.

She played it again. And again. And again.

By the time Im'mii found out what she'd been doing, weeks later, Sha'dar'dar's habit verged on a need. He gave her ten lashings to "teach her right from wrong." The next morning, he found her standing over his chest of wares yet again, bruised and aching, but recalcitrant. Concerned that the wayward child would cost him his thriving business, he took her to the Zezépfeni spaceport to find other work.

"A kindness to take you," he reminded her, for the third time that day.

Sha'dar'dar didn't believe him. He wanted her away from his goods. Fine—she wanted to be away, too, from him, from here. This was her chance. All the sound excavation companies, though owned by the High Council of the planet Zezépfeni, recruited labour from other planets. Ekwukwe and Órino-Rin were favoured sources for both labour and sound artefacts.

"You know why they choose us for this work?" Im'mii asked, as he led her to the spaceport. Ignoring the blaring recruitment calls from other excavation companies, he headed straight towards the one drawing people to Sauú3, the self-proclaimed leader in the field. "Ekwukwe and Órino-Rin have unique environments, filled with sites that have absorbed sound and hoarded it over centuries. We who were born on those planets have a natural affinity. We are easy to train, they say."

He let out a guffaw at this, as though the notion were ludicrous. Sha'dar'dar didn't laugh. She was too busy hoping it was true—that she would be easy to train. That the Zezépfenians would want her enough to keep her.

"Excavation pays well but it's brutal work," Im'mii said. "The Zezépfenians demand discipline and results. There is no place for weakness, especially in Sauú3. You probably won't survive."

Sha'dar'dar was barely listening, her gaze locked on the spacecraft docked at the port. Up, up, up . . . "Is that an excavation ship?"

"That hideous thing? No, that's the craft that takes recruits to the training facility on Órino-Rin. The excavation ships are much nicer. Smaller. Cleaner, too."

Up, up . . . Her echo had woken again, now that Im'mii

had cut off her supply of dangerous songs, and she could hear the others dancing on the fringes. Her sisters. Her brothers. Her parents. If she could get into the sky, to the stars, maybe that would be far enough. They couldn't follow her there, could they? Surely not. Surely even ghosts had limits.

"They say the very air on Órino-Rin is sharp enough to cut your echo away," said Im'mii. He mistook her silence for fear and went on, "Órino-Rin is always hungry, like those we never name. If you're not careful it will swallow you whole, echo and all. Keep your ears open, eh?"

But Sha'dar'dar was not afraid. She was elated. A place where the air would cut her echo away? Yes, yes, that was where she had to go. Up to Órino-Rin. The place without echoes.

Come dusk, Im'mii had gone and Sha'dar'dar stood in the queue with the other recruits boarding the ship. The recruitment officer, an Aq'pa who towered over the humans, moved down the line, taking names on a recording device. Although indigenous to Órino-Rin, Aq'pa were scattered across the binary star system. While others marveled at their height, strength or the way light rippled off their scales, Sha'dar'dar had always been struck by their double names, the first part a link to the material world, the second a link to Eh'wauizo, the world of the spirit.

When the officer approached her, signing *Name?* she froze. Her mind seemed to shut down as she stared into his black, glistening eyes.

Your name, child, he signed impatiently. *We're on a schedule.*

Sha'dar'dar said nothing. Her mind had gone blank. She couldn't even lift her hand to sign back.

The Aq'pa blinked and leaned in with a weary sigh. "Name," he whispered.

She trembled as a chill moved through her. Her mouth and eyes watered. If he had spoken louder, she might have lost control of her bladder. Aq'pa voices were deep and highly resonant. They had a unique effect on humans, each sound they uttered carrying the power of a minor incantation, and the species restricted themselves to Sign when dealing with humans.

It might have been the impact of the Aq'pa's voice or some delayed response to the events of recent weeks, but when she finally found her voice the name she gave was "Shad-Dari Seruwa." She pronounced her given name with her tongue between her teeth at the end of the first part and the start of the second: Shah-thuh-thah-ree. Like an Aq'pa name, though uttered without an ounce of the power it would have carried in that language, paired with a butchered form of her family name. Other recruits stared at her in confusion, wondering what game she was playing.

The recorder pinged, capturing her voice. The officer's eyes narrowed to slits. Sha'dar'dar could hardly breathe for fear. What sort of person would drop the echo in their name? It was sacrilege, like cutting off her own arm. Yet she felt no remorse. Only a fierce, dangerous thrill.

And no echoes. It seemed that the sheer rush of breaking the rules had banished the echoes as effectively as illicit songs, albeit for a shorter time. Maybe her dead relatives were shocked by her blasphemy. Maybe, if she continued to blaspheme, they would wash their hands of her at last.

She could see questions in the Aq'pa's eyes, behind a flash

of anger. It occurred to her that the words of her chosen name might mean something offensive in his tongue. Would he refuse to take her now?

Yet all he said was, *You're a fool*, and moved on.

On the ship, staring out into the blackness of space, Shad-Dari was born anew. She dreamed of what her life could be on Órino-Rin, far from the shackles of Ekwukwe. It seemed shiny with potential.

But the echoes remained.

It was said that Aq'pa names bound their bearers' souls and determined their fate, a spiritual contract between the Mother and her children. Shad-Dari would learn, shortly after landing on Órino-Rin, that in the Aq'pa tongue "shad" meant insatiable greed and "dari" was something like a walking shadow, a person who had no soul. A ghost. An inauspicious name, but she wore it like a talisman. It was the only thing, other than running away, that she had ever chosen for herself. Before it, life had been something that happened to her, barely requiring her participation, let alone her permission.

There was much to learn about excavating sound fragments. Shad-Dari had always known that sounds from all over the universe found their way to the unlikeliest places, carried in travellers' songs, physical artefacts, planetary debris, spells that lived in the bones of those who had cast or received them, satellite transmissions, dying wails locked in shipwrecks, prayers bound in temple ruins. Yet she had never imagined that the planets gobbled sound and hoarded it in tree roots, soil and mountain crevices, in water so deep no human could bear the pressure. She learned that sounds imbued with powerful emotion and matter-bending will lingered like echoes in the fabric of life, and that the right kind of magic could bring those sounds back, as loud as the day they were made.

She was thrilled to discover that the use of innate magic, echo magic for the Ekwukwe-born recruits like her, was banned during excavation jobs. Her home was on Órino-Rin now and her loyalty was to Zezépfeni. She put her voice signature on contract upon contract stating as much. Contracts to ensure compliance with Sauú3 regulations, contracts to prevent her from selling company secrets, contracts binding her to regular "spiritual support" from orange-robed Susu Nunyaa teachers, contracts to ensure that she replaced her "quaint but uncontrollable" echo magic with the "refined techniques" approved by the Zezépfeni Council.

Shad-Dari signed them all, selling a piece of her heritage with each contract, praying to the Mother that this treachery would be enough to turn the ghost echoes away. Why would they linger when she was no longer one of them? Why not go home, where they would be embraced?

And yet the echoes remained long after Sha'dar'dar ceased to exist, as though punishing her new incarnation was more important than finding peace in the hereafter.

Thankfully, Órino-Rin was full of dangerous, creative ways to silence one's demons. With her lucrative new job, Shad-Dari could afford to try them all.

The Aq'pa gathering was held in a tent—not the distinctive Tanti'ti shacks that often drifted overhead, but a simple temporary structure of metal and leather. Shad-Dari hid in a shadowy corner outside, wedged between the rocky side of a cliff and the taut surface of the tent. Her heart raced with anticipation as static crackled in the air—the sign of someone casting a concealment spell over the site to lock all the sound in.

A precaution. Not to protect the guests, but to protect human passersby. Gatherings like this were the only way Aq'pa who lived and worked among humans could properly relax, free to speak, laugh and even sing without fear of some fragile human fainting in the background. If they found Shad-Dari, the consequences would be . . . Well, she wasn't sure. As far as she knew, no one had ever been reckless enough to try to sneak in.

But desperate times called for desperate measures.

The Sauú3 Excavation Company had set up the Sauu'wa'en excavator training camp in the Tuu-Fani Region, far from Ducha'ga or any other city, to keep the trainees from distractions. Their efforts proved futile. The large trainee population attracted vendors hawking breathing masks, local delicacies and recycled worksuits, and then major Ts'jenene traders selling wares from across the five planets. Before long an entire settlement had sprung up around the camp, complete with its own seedy underbelly.

Shad-Dari had visited all the haunts and dabbled in all the

vices. At first they had lit her up, banishing the ghost echoes for days at a time. Now, in the final juzu of her three-juzu training, she seemed to have become immune to the effects. Her ghost echoes trailed her still, despite Im'mii's promise that the air of Órino-Rin would devour them. Órino-Rin was a finicky eater, it seemed, and Shad-Dari wasn't willing to wait until half her life had passed her by.

Pushing herself deeper into her hiding place, she slid to the ground so she could stretch out her legs a bit. She would never have found the site of the Aq'pa gathering—they changed locations constantly—if she hadn't been stalking an Aq'pa Sauú3 trainee for the better part of a month. Shad-Dari had followed her through the dark, ungazetted streets of Sauu'wa'en, echoes snapping at her heels.

She pressed herself against the tent, waiting. The only sound from inside was that of footsteps and muted music. They were waiting for confirmation that the concealment spell was in place. Any minute now . . . There. A whistle, low and drawn out, and then a sudden explosion of chattering voices.

Despite the cool air, Shad-Dari started to sweat beneath her breathing mask. Hives erupted along her limbs as the Aq'pa voices burrowed into her ears. A wave of vertigo struck and she slumped against the rock.

Sha-sha-sha . . . The echo was fainter already.

Shad-Dari swallowed the saliva pooling in her mouth and struggled to keep her eyes open. A little more. A little more and then she would summon the strength to crawl out of range before her insides began to bubble. The voices were like fingers caressing her spine, like insects crawling along the inside of her skull, like little people swimming in her blood, making it froth and hum with passion. Her body slid to the ground, trembling.

Sha . . . Almost gone. Almost.

Her tongue had died and become a bloated carcass between her teeth. Patches of darkness clouded her vision. She was slipping, slipping—

And then she was sliding across the ground, limbs dragged unceremoniously over puddles and rocks, until she felt the world bounce around her and snap back into place. The Aq'pa voices vanished. Now all she could hear was the wind and the barely controlled growl of some predator, which made her teeth chatter. A tetekute, no doubt. What a way to go.

She opened her eyes, her head clearing quickly now that she was out of earshot, and stared into a pair of black, fathomless eyes and a snarl baring jagged teeth. Not a tetekute, though perhaps an angry Aq'pa and a hungry feline weren't so different. It was the Sauú3 trainee Shad-Dari had followed.

You're lucky they always put someone on patrol or I'd be inside right now, while your organs liquefy here, the Aq'pa signed. *Why have you been following me?*

Shad-Dari flashed a weak smile and signed back, *Ah. You noticed.*

You think a human can follow an Aq'pa and not be noticed? Are you trying to kill yourself?

Part of herself, yes. But Shad-Dari wasn't going to admit that. She held out one hand. After a moment, the Aq'pa pulled her to her feet. *I'm just trying to have a little fun. I hear the sound of several Aq'pa talking at once can be orgasmic.*

Our voices are not for your entertainment. The Aq'pa released her with a grunt of disgust. *There's a place down the road if you want sii'swaar.*

Only the people of Órino-Rin would think to reserve a special name for illicit sounds. Sii'swaar—secret songs. Songs for the shadows, songs to inflict pain or evoke ecstasy, songs that made slaves of people.

I've tried that place, Shad-Dari replied.

There's another one—

I've tried them all.

The Aq'pa only glared at her. *You have broken both Sauú3 and Aq'pa regulations. I'm reporting you to the elders.*

Shad-Dari grabbed her arm. The Aq'pa's scales bit into her fingertips. "Don't," she begged. "Please. If you report me, I'll get kicked out of training."

You knew that when you came here.

"I have owo. How much will it take?" The Aq'pa growled again, giving Shad-Dari goosebumps. Ah. Wrong tactic. Shad-Dari put on a smile and signed, *What's your name?*

Bed-Shek.

"A pleasure, Bed-Shek. I'm Shad-Dari."

Everybody knows your ridiculous made-up name. You're one of those types. Bed-Shek's lip curled in revulsion. *The ones with an Aq'pa fetish.*

"Maybe." Shad-Dari grinned shamelessly and then, for reasons she couldn't quite decipher, added, "My birth name is Sha'dar'dar."

The Aq'pa stared at her in surprise. *Why would you tell me that?*

Shad-Dari shrugged, switching back to Sign. *It doesn't mean anything. Just sounds strung together.*

Bed-Shek scoffed, as though sensing the lie in the words. *Your name is your nature. Your fate. You came here in a mask, and you just showed me what's beneath it. A stranger.*

Shad-Dari heard the unasked question and chose to ignore it. Maybe she felt she owed Bed-Shek for taking a false Aq'pa name and disrespecting their culture. Maybe she wanted Bed-Shek to know something about her, something real, even if it was something Shad-Dari had discarded. But this wasn't the sort of discussion she was ready to have.

Look, tell me what you want in exchange for your silence, she signed. *Anything.*

Bed-Shek turned away and started back towards the tent.

"No, please! What do you want?" Shad-Dari shouted. She ran after the Aq'pa, overtook her and blocked her path. *Please. Anything. Anything. I'll never do this again. Please.*

Bed-Shek was silent for a moment. *Give me your spot on the Zezépfeni practice dig.*

Are you joking? I worked months of extra hours to get that spot!

The Aq'pa cocked her head.

Desperate times . . . With a sigh, Shad-Dari relented. *Fine. The spot is yours.*

Bed-Shek lingered for a moment, then said, *There are easier ways to die. I'll show you if you promise to leave me all your slots on the best digs. I'll even pretend to cry at the funeral.*

It took a moment to ascertain that the Aq'pa was joking, and then Shad-Dari laughed.

The day of her final exam, Shad-Dari stood in the training hall, a large drum on the ground before her. She wore thick leather bracelets on each arm, studded with glowing sound crystals. A few steps ahead, the instructor held a glass orb in their hands. The orb vibrated, making the instructor's fingers tremble. Only a small rubber stopper kept the sound inside from escaping.

Harnessing the energy contained in the crystals on her wrists, Shad-Dari sent it forward with a flick of her finger. The stopper popped free, dropping to the ground with a bounce. She quickly contained the song with a film of pure sound energy, then held the film in place by pressing her thumb against her forefinger, as though pinching a thread. She began to pull, first with one hand, then the other, drawing the song towards her drum.

The instructor nodded their approval. So far, so good.

Sha . . . shaaaaaaa . . . .

Shad-Dari gritted her teeth, wondering how it was possible that no one else could hear the echoes when they were so bloody loud. It didn't matter. She would soon quell them. While the eyes of the instructor and the watching trainees remained on her pulling motion and the vague crackle of static that ran along the edges of the song, Shad-Dari sent a sliver of energy in a different direction, using only her left little finger. One tiny flick and a line peeled away from the rest of the song, curling in on itself like a ribbon before floating through the air for everyone to hear.

Mother, make me wiser than the child who went before. A complete line, perfect, not a word or note out of place.

Some fool gasped, making the rest of the song judder. Shad-Dari frowned, sweat beading on her forehead, but maintained her grip. She widened her eyes, trying her best to look anxious and scared, while on the inside triumph bloomed.

She had been practicing that single flick for months. The piece she had sliced away was far too big, but it was only a test. Next time she would take a fraction of a fraction, less than a word, less than a syllable. She would steal pieces of the rarest, most powerful sounds in the world and put them in her pocket, and the treachery alone would silence her overbearing ghosts for weeks.

Depositing what remained of the song into the drum and sealing it, Shad-Dari exhaled and turned to face the aghast instructor.

"What did you do?" they murmured in horror.

"I'm sorry," Shad-Dari said, injecting a tremor into her voice. "It was an accident. I don't know how—"

"I've never seen someone do that. Cut a song like that, with such precision . . ."

"By accident," Shad-Dari persisted.

The instructor nodded. "Of course. It must have been." Their face was clouded with doubt, but the alternative was unthinkable. Who would mutilate sound on purpose? Why? "I will have to take off points."

Shad-Dari lowered her head in a show of frustration. "But I worked so hard! Please—"

"Don't worry," the instructor said. "We all make mistakes

and your technique was otherwise excellent. You will still pass."

It was only then that Shad-Dari allowed herself to smile.

She loved Órino-Rin. She loved the mist that coiled around bodies and buildings in an eerily serpentine fashion, the grating air that chafed her lungs raw each time she dared breathe deeply. She loved the storms that raged like a tantrum. She loved her training, relishing the opportunity to learn to wield sound energy without tapping into her echo magic. Most of all, she loved the space. No walls pressing in on all sides, deep in the stone bowels of the world. No siblings and cousins to crowd around her, competing for food and attention. Here, she lived so far above the planet's surface that she could almost imagine that it didn't exist, that there were only the mountains floating in the clouds, peaks kissing the suns.

Other trainees tried to befriend her. Some were curious about the Ekwukwe girl with the knockoff Aq'pa name. Others admired her focus. Unfortunately for her peers, she had no interest in making friends with anyone but Bed-Shek, perhaps because the Aq'pa treated her with cool civility bordering on disdain. Shad-Dari loved a challenge.

On their last day in Sauu'wa'en, before they were due to ship out, they received their assignments. Thrilled to learn that she and Bed-Shek would be on the same crew, Shad-Dari sought the Aq'pa out. She found her on her way to the instructors' quarters. She fell into step with her, though she had to jog to keep up with Bed-Shek's long stride.

"We're on the same crew, did you hear?"

Not for long, the Aq'pa replied, her expression stony. *I'm going to ask for reassignment.*

"Why? Our first job is just outside Ducha'ga! I've never been in the city."

I saw what you did in the exam today. It was no accident.

Shad-Dari shrugged. "So?"

So? Bed-Shek stopped to glare at Shad-Dari. *This is the problem with you. You think it's fun to take needless risks. If you pull that kind of stunt on a dig you could get your whole crew killed!*

"You think I'd put you in harm's way?" Shad-Dari shook her head. "I might risk *my* life, but not anyone else's."

Fool. If you suffer, the whole crew suffers. I'm not interested in losing my job because you can't control yourself. Bed-Shek's eyes flashed. *If we work together, no more risks. No more sneaking out, no more sii'swaar.*

Shad-Dari didn't hesitate. "Done." Keeping her habits a secret from her own crew would add a level of risk that heightened the experience.

Swear it.

"I swear on the Mother."

Liars swear on the Mother all the time. Swear on something closer, something you can never betray. Swear on your echo.

Shad-Dari almost recoiled, before she saw the opportunity. It was a fair assumption—the echo was a deep, sacred part of all those from Ekwukwe. Well, almost all. The loophole was so perfect, she could crawl through it with her eyes closed.

Another person might have paused to consider the implications, but Shad-Dari wasn't one to waste a gift.

"I swear on my echo and the echoes of my whole family."

The tension left Bed-Shek's face instantly. She nodded.

It would take her three juzu to let her guard down enough to call Shad-Dari her friend. It would only take Shad-Dari three weeks to break her promise.

3.

THE QUIET was so wonderful, she wished she could drink it.

Her body hadn't stopped aching—Mah Mmi'ino was right, she might have pushed it too far—but the ghosts were still gone. She could hear the ship's engines. She could hear the faint sloshing of liquid in the orbs encasing each of the Mahu Mahadii.

Shad-Dari watched the Mahu Mahadii descend the steep back ramp out of the ship. The tank they lived in while on the ship was too heavy to bring to the surface, but the orbs, made of a translucent, rubbery substance that stretched as needed to accommodate them, floated above the ground, keeping their occupants safe from any dangers that might lurk on the surface.

Whenever the crew visited a new site, the Mahu Mahadii insisted on disembarking before the others so they could have time to acclimatize.

"Please follow us closely," Shad-Dari said.

The creatures didn't respond. They probably thought her concern obviously unfounded. They were far better able to protect themselves than she was. Shad-Dari closed the ramp, left the cargo hold and made her way back to the bridge.

The *Nuseh-Tor* was one of the smallest ships in the Sauú3

fleet, which made it perfect for both off and on-world travel. Most ships had a crew of ten, but when assigned the ship, Shad-Dari had taken advantage of the *Nuseh-Tor's* size to request a smaller team. Ten people crawling around on her ship—technically Sauú3's ship, but such details were irrelevant—was not her idea of a peaceful working environment.

She passed the infirmary, where the Susu Nunyaa-approved uroh-ogi had chosen to remain cloistered, too stuck-up to mix with the commoners. The scholar-priests sent a different healer for every job, for reasons they didn't see fit to explain. Shad-Dari had always suspected it was to prevent the uroh-ogi from bonding with the crew and shifting loyalties. She rarely bothered to learn the uroh-ogis' names—what was the point, when they'd be gone in under a week?

She reached the ship's bridge in time to catch her crew gossiping as Fafali completed the landing sequence.

"I'm not joking!" Kga'arah was saying, pulling on her boots. "It was so bad that some of the Susu Nunyaa lost their minds and someone even died after hearing the fragments."

Rori'iro laughed. "Nonsense! Those are just rumours. The Susu Nunyaa have been listening to fragments forever. The sounds don't affect them the way they affect normal people."

"They ARE BUILT for it," Fafali agreed, his voice fluctuating in volume.

Born among pirates who rode the harshest storms to harness their sounds, he had long since lost the ability to modulate his voice. He would have used Sign, were his hands not busy wielding the sound energy that powered the ship.

Bed-Shek scoffed, her scales standing on end to release

built-up tension from the journey. *Susu Nunyaa are human. Of course they're affected. They just don't want us to know.*

"I hope you fools remembered to turn off communications before slandering our masters," Shad-Dari said. "I think some of you are still drunk from last night."

"Ah, was it not you who threw the party?" Rori'iro winced as he tugged a helmet over his bruised face—a souvenir from the kartel members he had taunted the night before. Shad-Dari noted, with a glimmer of pride, that the incriminating tattoo still adorned his neck.

"You want more bruises to complement those ones?" she countered, but the boy only laughed.

The engines fell silent. Nothing but mist was visible through the screen. Shad-Dari went to the ship's exit, yanked the lever to open the ramp, then turned to face her approaching crew as she put on her own helmet. In addition to helping them breathe, the helmets contained their radios and were shielded with concealment spells, ensuring that their speech didn't get sucked into the atmosphere. Only Bed-Shek would still have to rely only on Sign.

Kga'arah handed out the large drums they would use to contain the fragments they unearthed. Her scales lying flat once more, Bed-Shek waited until the ramp struck the ground, then headed out first. Standard protocol, as her physiology offered greater protection from extreme conditions on the meridian and her powerful senses would alert her to danger the humans might miss. The uroh-ogi hadn't bothered to come out. Shad-Dari stifled her annoyance—that sort of arrogance was the Susu

Nunyaa way. Taking a drum from Kga'arah, she slid her arms into the straps and tightened the harness round her waist.

The crew waited in tense silence for Bed-Shek to give the all-clear, staring into the dark mist below. They had explored sisu'um before, larger sites mapped by previous generations. This particular site was a recent discovery, virgin territory as far as excavation was concerned. Shad-Dari knew only that the Sauú3 executives—shadowy figures who never showed their faces—had pulled strings to wrestle control of the site from other excavation companies.

Bed-Shek emerged from the mist, her gait steady, but the set of her jaw told Shad-Dari something was wrong.

"Do we need extra protection?" Shad-Dari asked.

The Aq'pa shook her head. *The site is as we were told. Thick mist, many silence pockets. But we have company.*

Kga'arah cursed. "Of course Sauú3 would choose today to run inspections."

It's not Sauú3. Bed-Shek came up the ramp. *It's a delegation from Zezépfeni; two Council representatives and a Susu Nunyaa. An important one, too, one of their senior inatani.*

This time, they all cursed. Susu Nunyaa teachers and Council reps didn't belong on digs.

"Did they say what they wanted?" Shad-Dari asked.

You think I got close enough to ask? Bed-Shek gave her a look. *Any ideas?*

Shad-Dari had a few ideas and none of them sat well with her. Either the Council had come to monitor the site, perhaps because there was something different about it—and differences spelled trouble in this line of work—or they had come to monitor the crew.

"Give me a moment," she said. "Let me see what I can find out."

She hurried back to her cabin, knowing the crew would assume she was going to make contact with one of her friends in Saúú3 management. Her thoughts raced. Her crew performed well. They had just found the oldest fragments on record. If anything, they should be getting more freedom, not less. Had her employers finally realized she was stealing from them?

Reaching her cabin, she rifled through the wooden chest where she kept her personal effects and withdrew three drums containing stolen sounds she had not used yet. Slipping them into an empty pocket, she returned to the crew. If the delegation searched the ship, at least they wouldn't find anything incriminating. She would dispose of the drums somewhere on the site. She doubted that they would risk searching her person until after the dig.

"Did you learn anything?" Kga'arah asked.

Shad-Dari shook her head. "I couldn't get through, but there must be more to this site than they told us. Maybe they think we'll find more fragments from the Seeding down there. We should be extra careful."

As soon as the Mahu Mahadii caught up, Bed-Shek led the crew through the mist by the light of their bracelets, belts and boots, all studded with crystals, plus the battery in Kga'arah's hand, a dodecahedral honeycomb with crystals nestled in each little hollow. As the crew moved through the silence pockets, any sound that might have arisen was sucked right out of the air. Even their footsteps made no noise as they moved over wet leaves and grass. Visibility in the pockets was poor for the humans—their light sources flickered and faded as the sound energy that fed them disappeared into the silence—but Bed-Shek was the ideal leader, her eyes built for the planet's moody mist. And then, once they had moved past the pocket, light and sound returned.

Ahead of the party stretched a mass of trees, stunted and scantily clad in long, wet leaves that draped like loose threads over their branches. They came upon the delegation, clustered around a ball of garish, yellow-tinged light. The Council members were clothed in dark robes of a colour Shad-Dari couldn't quite identify—burgundy or perhaps brown—while the Susu Nunyaa wore the traditional orange robes, edges appearing green in the light of the crystals. Their expressions were inscrutable behind their helmets.

"Greetings, elders," Shad-Dari said, inclining her head in a polite bow. "Welcome to Órino-Rin. My name is Shad-Dari, captain of the *Nuseh-Tor* and head of this crew."

"We know of you, Shad-Dari," the Susu Nunyaa said.

"Apologies for keeping you waiting—we weren't informed that you would be joining us. We would have made preparations, brought extra gear—"

"No need." The orange-clad inatani seemed to be the only one inclined to speak. "Proceed as usual. We are only here to observe."

"Of course. You're welcome, though I will have to ask that you allow my crew to go first, for your own safety."

"Naturally."

"Is there anything in particular you're looking for? If we know, we'll be better able to assist."

With a small, cryptic smile, the inatani simply waved the crew forward.

Bed-Shek shot Shad-Dari a wary glance before leading them deeper into the forest. The Aq'pa was nervous about the unexpected visitors. Shad-Dari couldn't blame her. They had been subjected to many inspections over the juzu, but always at the hands of haughty Sauú3 officers that they knew how to handle. These three were another animal altogether. Not to mention, if something happened to them during the dig, Shad-Dari would be held responsible.

They moved through the dark, dense forest, weaving in and out of the silences. A feeling of dread settled over Shad-Dari, and not just because of the sii'swaar in her pocket or the piercing gazes of the "observers" behind her. There was something about this place. Something sinister, beyond the pockets of silence. It felt like the sort of place hopeless people might go to die.

At the edge of the lake, just before the largest silence pocket, Shad-Dari raised her hand to stop the procession. Dead trees rose out of the water like the twisted soldiers of some phantom army, arms reaching out to grab the enemy. The Mahu Mahadii hovered high above the crew, just beyond the pockets, but they would have to pass through the biggest one to go below the lake's surface.

"How deep do we need to travel?" Shad-Dari asked them.

They were quiet for a moment, evaluating their surround-ings, and then their reply came over her earpiece.

"To start with, seven cycles."

Seven cycles—the distance the Mahu Mahadii could travel in seven paces, with a pace being each time their tentacles touched the ground. A subjective and infuriating mode of measurement, as the creatures could differ in size from newborns as tiny as pebbles to elders that dwarfed the *Nuseh-Tor*. Shad-Dari did a quick estimation, based on the average size of the Mahu Mahadii present. Seven cycles would be roughly twenty-eight metres below the surface. To start with.

Shad-Dari nodded. "Aim for thirty down and counting. Drums open! Remember, choose your positions well. If anyone stumbles into a silent pocket while carrying a fragment, and we lose it, I will throttle them myself. Bed-Shek, I need you in the water. As far as they'll let you go."

Bed-Shek had already removed her boots, freeing her webbed feet, and waded in under the bobbing orbs. She would follow the Mahu Mahadii's trail to avoid the pockets.

"Rori, on my right. Kga'arah, on the bank. Battery on standby. Elders, please step back. Our work is bound to disturb the water."

To her relief, the guests didn't argue. They moved away from the water's edge, giving the excavators room to work. A silence pocket wasn't, in itself, a problem for excavators—although no sound, and therefore no magic or tech—could exist within them, the crew could work along the periphery of the pockets. The true challenge of a sisu'um lay in the number of pockets. Many were the size of a room, others the size of a fist. They dotted the forest like drops of aural paint splattered by a capricious god, but clung only to the surface, leaving the sky and lakebed clear. Moving around them was one thing. Moving around them while wielding sound magic, to unearth priceless sound artefacts, was another thing entirely.

The seven orbs came to a stop above the middle of the lake, right inside the pocket, and then dropped as one into the water. Bed-Shek surfaced, treading water not far from where the Mahu Mahadii had descended. From the way she kept her arms tucked in tight, Shad-Dari guessed that the Aq'pa was navigating the soundspace between two silences. It would be a tricky dig, if that was all the wiggle room they had. Where and when could she dispose of the stolen sounds in her pockets? Would the chance present itself at all? Excitement licked at her thoughts, but Shad-Dari turned her focus back to the place where the Mahu Mahadii had descended, keeping her gaze on the water until the ripples had smoothed out. Her fingers rested against her thighs, flexing and stretching in preparation.

The wait didn't bother her when her ghosts were quiet, as they were now. Anticipation curled in her belly. What would they find this time? Fragments of spells from long-lost rituals? Songs no one had sung in centuries, or even millennia? What delicious chaos would such sound wreak upon her body, once Mah Mmi'ino got to work? Shad-Dari couldn't wait to find out.

A massive bubble rose to the surface and popped soundlessly. Another. Soon the surface came alive, frothing with a fury, indicating that whatever emerged would be heavy to carry and low in resonance.

"Bed-Shek!"

The Aq'pa raised her hand and nodded. The sound erupted from below, an inaudible force that sent water splashing so far it drenched Shad-Dari and Rori'iro, who braced themselves but held their ground. The splash just missed Kga'arah. None of them dared to shift position, not at this critical moment. A frisson of Mahu Mahadii current lit up the fragment for a fraction of a second, long enough for Bed-Shek to sheath it in raw energy and then begin lifting it up and over the largest silence pocket.

Shad-Dari raised her arms and sent her own power up with gentle twisting motions of her fingers, manoevering it over the pocket so she could help with the load. Teeth gritted with effort, the two of them drew the fragment above their heads and across the water, following the Sauú3 protocol. Fill the furthest drums first, the ones closest to the ship, in case trouble struck and they had to make a quick getaway. Leaving an excavator behind was acceptable. Leaving a fragment behind was not.

It was slow, arduous work, steering the sound-sealed fragment in a neat arc, careful not to let it fall. And then Shad-Dari felt something brush past her leg in the water. Something huge. Something with pincers. Suddenly the sisu'um smelled—the word came to her in a burst of bizarre clarity—red. Without warning, the entire lake seemed to transform into a burial ground, ripe with the stench of decay. Her head swam. What was this?

"Shad, you're slipping!" Kga'arah cried out.

Shad-Dari looked up to see that she had brought the fragment perilously close to the silence. Panic made her send a burst of power forth, bringing the fragment back into alignment. She risked a glance at Bed-Shek. The Aq'pa's face was tense. Shad-Dari's legs trembled with stunned fear. Only Bed-Shek's physical strength had kept the fragment aloft—if it had been anyone else, they would have lost the fragment to the silence. She had never lost a fragment in the decade she had been an excavator. Such a loss would be the end of her vocation. Her life.

Once the fragment was close enough, Kga'arah took on some of the weight as the three of them eased the fragment into her drum and pushed it into the bottom compartment. The concealment spell Kga'arah had begun to weave set the moment the fragment was in. It would keep it contained while she left the drum open to collect the next.

A soft, low growl came over Shad-Dari's comms, setting her teeth on edge and making her legs tremble all over again. She looked towards the Aq'pa.

What in the Mother's name was that? Bed-Shek demanded, her gestures tense. *Are you all right?*

"I'm fine," Shad-Dari said. "And I'm sorry. That was completely unacceptable. There was something . . ." Her knees threatened to buckle, but she forced herself to remain upright. Her crew needed to see her strong. Capable. In control. She looked down into the water, but saw nothing there. "It won't happen again. Prep for the next one."

The others exchanged concerned glances, but turned their focus back to the water. Shad-Dari glanced at the delegation. They paid no attention to the excavators—their eyes were fixed on the spot in the lake where the fragment had come from. What were they expecting to find down there? What did they know?

It didn't matter—soon enough the mystery would be

solved. Shad-Dari realized she might not get another chance to dump her stolen goods. She would fling them into the silence, where they would vanish like vapour. Where they could do no harm. Another bubble had appeared. She had to act now, before attention shifted back to her. She reached into her worksuit, opened the three little drums containing the stolen sounds and directed their contents into the water in front of her—into one of the silences. They were swallowed instantly, without as much as a whisper. Her shoulders sagged with relief. No evidence, no crime. For now, anyway. Her gaze shifted to Kga'arah and the drum on her back. Shad-Dari would need to find a way to siphon a sliver of sound from the drum before it was sealed. She couldn't risk doing it during the excavation itself—not with those treacherous silences surrounding her.

The crew captured the next fragment, and the next. Shad-Dari kept her focus this time, ignoring the sense of foreboding. After several minutes of calm, she frowned. There were no more bubbles. The water was still as glass.

For a terrifying moment she wondered whether the stolen sounds had fallen beyond the silence pocket after all. Was it possible? Had they found their way down to where the artefacts were? Perhaps the Mahu Mahadii knew what she had done . . .

"Bed-Shek, can you see below?" she called out.

The Aq'pa shook her head. They waited. And waited. The Mahu Mahadii's ancient magic burrowed deep to call up the sounds of the past. It sometimes took a while to get started, but once they had unearthed a fragment they typically made quick progress. Something was definitely wrong.

Shad-Dari chewed her lip. "Go."

Bed-Shek sank below the surface.

"They hate it when we disrupt their work," Kga'arah murmured.

"You think I don't know that?" Shad-Dari heard an irksome throat-clearing in her ear, through her comms. Mother save her. "Yes, elders?"

"Have our amphibian friends encountered a difficulty?"

Shad-Dari stifled the urge to march over to where the Susu Nunyaa stood on the bank and smother her with her own robes. "I've sent my best swimmer down to investigate. I'm sure—"

The lake exploded. Massive waves rose up and crashed upon them.

"Retreat!" Shad-Dari shouted. "Get the elders to safety!"

Kga'arah, who was closest to the guests, half ran, half swam in their direction. Rori'iro treaded water, making no effort to get out.

"Rori! Get back to the ship!"

"I think I saw Bed-Shek!" His voice shook with terror. "She looked . . . She's hurt!"

Hurt? Bed-Shek? Shad-Dari couldn't even imagine such a thing—compared to fragile human flesh the Aq'pa might as well be made of stone. And yet there she was, a figure floating in the turbulent waters, the current tossing her to and fro, scales glowing in a way that looked entirely unnatural.

For a moment Shad-Dari wondered why Bed-Shek was wearing a barkcloth tunic and trousers instead of her sturdy worksuit, why the scales on her hands had been replaced by human skin, why her feet were in boots when she'd been barefoot. And then the mist cleared and she realized she was imagining things. Guilt rose inside her like bile as she swam to her injured friend. Rori'iro reached her first.

"Get her to the fishing boat!" said Shad-Dari.

The words were swallowed by the silence, which was just as well, as they made no sense. She had no idea why she'd uttered them. Her mind felt strange and slippery, a tangle of wriggling thoughts. The only thing she knew for sure was that this was her doing. She and her sii'swaar had put her crew, her friend, in danger, just as Bed-Shek had warned her would happen, all those years ago when they were trainees.

She was Captain of the *Nuseh-Tor* first and foremost, beholden to her masters, and there was still a job to be done. Shad-Dari did what she did best. She folded her emotions up and packed them away.

She and Rori'iro carried the unconscious Bed-Shek out of the water and lay her down on the bank. The orbs resurfaced behind them, electricity flashing furiously. Shad-Dari could feel the Mahu Mahadii's distress like an ache in her muscles, a vibration that set her teeth on edge. She didn't want to deal with their strangeness now, not when Bed-Shek lay unresponsive on the ground.

"Get her to the ship," she instructed Rori'iro, then turned back towards the water to deal with the Mahu Mahadii. "What happened down there?"

For a moment all she could glean from them was a frenzied hum. They were afraid. Or angry. Or in pain—she couldn't tell.

"Slower, please!"

"Sounds," they said. "Foreign sounds that should not be

there. Went too deep. Opened the wrong doors. We will not risk it. We will return to the ship."

Shad-Dari went cold. So it *was* the fragments she had thrown in. They had done something—triggered something. Something bad. But the Mahu Mahadii didn't realise that it was her doing—not yet, at least. "We can take a break and try again."

"No. We will not risk it."

Shad-Dari stared at them. "But there are still artefacts down there. You know the rules. We can't leave until we have—"

"Your rules are of no consequence."

The world seemed to spin a little, everything turning on its head. Shad-Dari closed her eyes, gathering her composure, then glanced over her shoulder at the Zezépfeni delegation, who had drawn closer once more now that the waters had calmed. "All right. Please wait here. Give me a moment to explain the situation to my elders. It's a complicated—"

The Mahu Mahadii floated past her as if she had not spoken, heading back to the ship.

"What's going on?" the inatani demanded, striding forward, her features creased in disapproval.

With a deep breath to steel herself, Shad-Dari turned to face the Susu Nunyaa. "The excavation appears to have triggered some sort of reaction which unsettled our friends. I'm sorry, but we'll have to cut the dig short and come back another day."

"No." The Susu Nunyaa smiled. "We will proceed."

"One of my crew is injured."

"You have an uroh-ogi. Tell the Mahu Mahadii to continue."

Shad-Dari let out a burst of shocked laughter. "With

respect, no one tells the Mahu Mahadii to do anything. They're not employees of Sauú3, or citizens of Zezépfeni. We have three new fragments. They have done their part, according to the terms of the alliance."

"Hmm," the inatani murmured, her smile still pasted on her face. "Thank you for explaining the alliance to me; I had forgotten how it works."

Fury blossomed in Shad-Dari's chest, but she forced herself to remain calm. "I didn't mean—"

"We will proceed. The amphibians have surely drawn more fragments close enough to the surface for you to carry them the rest of the way. You're an excavator, yes? So excavate."

For a moment, Shad-Dari was too stunned to speak. She glanced at the other two delegates, who had still not found their voices, then at Kga'arah, who shrugged. The Mahu Mahadii might be done for the day, but the excavators had no choice.

Kga'arah stepped forward. Shad-Dari shook her head. She was the risk-taker, after all, and this entire mess was her fault. If anyone should go down there, it should be her.

"Let me come with you," said Kga'arah, but Shad-Dari shook her head again.

"If I can't carry the fragments, I'll call for you. Stay close and keep Bed-Shek's drum open."

It had been a long time since Shad-Dari had been afraid. Not the delicious rush of adrenalin she felt when she stole a fragment, the thrill of possibly being caught. No, that came with the certainty of silencing her echoes. *This* fear was a primal thing, an animal trapped inside her, howling to be let out. This was the fear of the unknown, of whatever lurked in the water. Of finding herself on the other side, trapped with the ghosts forever. Her head swam again, making her stumble as she waded into the water.

"I'm fine," she called out, pre-empting Kga'arah's question.

Whatever had unsettled the Mahu Mahadii was still in the water. Her stolen sounds alone would not have affected them that way, but if the sounds had, as the Mahu Mahadii said, "opened the wrong doors" . . . What did that mean? What was behind those wrong doors? Maybe that was what had knocked Bed-Shek unconscious. The deeper Shad-Dari went, the stronger her foreboding grew.

Turn back. Turn back and look at Kga'arah. You'll regret it if you don't.

She followed the silent instruction from her own voice, even though it seemed strange and sentimental. Her gaze met Kga'arah's and she felt a fleeting, frantic urge to see the others, especially Bed-Shek. How many juzu had they known each other? Too many, Bed-Shek would say, and Shad-Dari would laugh.

This is ridiculous, she thought. I'm not going to die. It was a prayer. A challenge, perhaps.

No. No, not today.

Her voice . . . yet not her voice.

She plunged underwater, swimming as fast as she could. There was definitely something in the water, something other than the dark, menacing trunks of the dead trees and the oppressive silence. Something . . . hungry. This was what her stolen sounds had unleashed. She could feel it pull her in like a whirlpool, a gaping hole seeking unwitting prey. It was huge. It had to be—the water had started to swirl towards it.

How could she possibly excavate around this mysterious presence? Would she be able to identify the remaining artefacts without the Mahu Mahadii's current lighting them up for her?

The lake exploded again. The water pressure seemed to double, until her organs felt as though they were trying to escape through her skin. She could hear things. Screaming and crying and other things, whispered things. Spells? Prayers? She couldn't tell, but the water was filled with them. So this was where all the sounds had gone. This was where they were hiding. Hiding from the silences, she wondered? From the excavators? From the delegates?

Bodies appeared and then dissolved before her eyes. Something that looked like a robot floated past, lights flickering in its skull before it shattered into dust.

Then she saw it, the fishing boat she had mentioned earlier, floating above beside a limp body, barkcloth clothes billowing, heavy boots weighing it down. She knew it was the body of someone small, someone fragile, and when she swam closer she saw that the body had the face of her little sister. Kefi.

Something else was in the water now, mist in an orb, flickering with electricity. Why were the Mahu Mahadii back? She wanted to tell them she could do it alone, but the orb split open and the creature spread its many, many tentacles and she saw that ah! It had a mouth, after all, a big yawning hole that drew her in, and in, and in . . .

Her chest burst into flames. She couldn't breathe. Or she could, but her lungs were full of water instead of air. The Mahu

Mahadii's mouth closed over her, sealing her in—Mother, everything in all the worlds was hungry—and her skin was burning, breaking down, disintegrating in the silent darkness.

That was when she realized she was dying.

4.

THERE WERE echoes in the water. They were what woke her, with their relentless pulsing through the cold crush, long-dead children still crying for attention. She resisted, at first—let them cry, they would grow up and learn that life cared nothing for their tears—but then she remembered what resisting would mean. Fading. Dying. Joining them at last.

And the possibility was so monstrous that her remaining will grabbed hold of those echoes and rode them all the way to consciousness.

Her eyes opened, her body yielding to the terror of burning lungs and water, water, water. Nothing else existed. There was only cold and pressure and thrashing desperation. Which way was up? Which way, which way? Was there "up" at all, or was all the world water? She fought, eyes wide, mouth closed, lungs screaming, even though her foe was too vast and detached to notice that it had trapped her, let alone bother to set her free.

She was on Zezépfeni, somehow. In the fathomless maw of Meshe-Shekhiiyem. And she thought, as darkness slid ever closer, that maybe she should have been better-behaved as a child, more reverent, less rebellious. Maybe Meshe-Shekhiiyem would see her if she were a true believer. Maybe the sacred sea would let her live.

She was sinking. There was "up," after all. That way, drifting out of reach. Her body was a throbbing, ravaged thing, all pain and hunger. And resignation. She was going to end here. Not even on her beloved Órino-Rin, not even on her home ground of Ekwukwe, but here, on the planet that had bought her soul. Well, perhaps it was fitting. Perhaps her bones had been part of the transaction, one of the clauses hidden in the barely audible terms and conditions.

And then the water came alive around her, a symphony of crackling current and a hundred thousand tentacles. The Mahu Mahadii. She had forgotten about them. Were they here, also? Had she brought them? Their tentacles coiled around her limbs. Death by Mahu Mahadii would be better than drowning, surely. Would they rip her apart? Pump her full of current? Devour her? Again?

They did none of those things. They raced her to the surface—she didn't know the creatures could move with such speed—and cast her out so she could no longer defile their precious ocean. She landed on her back in the sand, coughing up water. For some time, all she could do was lie there, blinking into the pink sky, gulping in air.

She was alive. And there were no echoes.

Slowly, Shad-Dari peeled her body off the beach and stood up. She was just outside the city of Zezelam. The boundary loomed in the distance, a wall of stone humming with sound magic to keep the meteors and unpredictable climate at bay. She remembered being swallowed . . . Had the Mahu Mahadii caried her in its belly all the way back to the ship, and flown them here? Why hadn't it regurgitated her on the ship? Thrown her back with the others? The Mahu Mahadii had no interest in helping other species, so why save her at all?

Pointless questions, she knew. Shad-Dari looked out over the water. The creatures were gone, off to carry on their lives until the next time they were required to honour their agreement with Zezépfeni. "Thank you," she whispered, and then walked towards the boundary. She had to get back to base and find her crew. Find Bed-Shek. She could contact Ducha'ga from the Sauú3 headquarters in Zezelam and get on the next ship back to Órino-Rin.

When she reached the gate, a small door opened to admit her into the holding room. Two guards stood on the other side, their expressions impassive. They had changed their uniforms, for some reason—the familiar mother-of-pearl shades of their sleek, tech-fortified armour replaced with garments of thick, simple brown leather. They carried shields. Cumbersome. Impractical. Ridiculous.

"Greetings, brothers. Is there a costume party?" Shad-Dari eyed their uniforms with confusion.

The guards glowered and pointed her wordlessly to the disinfection chamber. Raising her arms in surrender, she entered.

A moment later, jets of liquid attacked her from the walls, making her splutter in shock. The water had a vague, bitter tang to it. Why they were using water at all, instead of aural cleansing pods, was another mystery. A gust of warm air followed the unceremonious, unwanted bath, and then a guard opened the door of the chamber to let her out.

"What in the name of the Mother is going on?" she sputtered.

"Did something happen here? Why have you reverted to these archaic techniques?"

The guard's expression remained impassive as he tapped the entry log embedded in the wall. "I don't know what you mean. Identify yourself and state your business, please."

"The worksuit doesn't give it away?" Shad-Dari heaved an impatient sigh. "My name is Shad-Dari Seruwa. I'm a Sauú3 excavator, obviously." She pointed at the rings in her ears indicating her status. "Captain. Of the *Nuseh-Tor*, to be specific. I'm stranded and need to get back to base, so if you could hurry things along—"

The guard tapped the log again and a click sounded, followed by Shad-Dari's voice. "Shad-Dari Seruwa. Sauú3 excavator. Captain of the *Nuseh-Tor*."

"And what is Sauú3?" the guard enquired.

Shad-Dari blinked, and then chuckled. "Ah! You're absolutely right. I should have presented my ID. Forgive me—I almost drowned and my thoughts are somewhat duller than usual."

Reaching under the top part of her suit, Shad-Dari unzipped the little pocket where excavators kept their ID recordings. They were required by law to carry them at all times, so their corpses could be identified if they died in the line of duty. She withdrew a device about the size of her thumb and flicked the switch on its side.

A mechanical voice rang out clearly in the holding room. "This recording is intended to identify the bearer, employee and property of the Sauú3 Excavation Company, Zezépfeni's premier provider of sound excavation services, as required by

Article 7 of the Sauúti-tongue Recovery Charter. The bearer indemnifies Sauú3 of any consequences resulting from loss of or damage to this recording. Name: Shad-Dari Seruwa. Rank: Captain. Ship: *Nuseh-Tor*. Planet of Origin: Ekwukwe. Base planet of operations: Órino-Rin. Please note that The Sauú3 Company does not engage in rescue missions or pay ransom for employees. In the event of the bearer's death or incapacity, kindly return the bearer, along with any sound fragments in their possession, to The Sauú3 Company headquarters on Kwartey Island, Zezelam. Failure to do so will lead to prosecution. Sauú3. Preserving the past to ensure the future."

The guard frowned. He beckoned to one of his fellows and they conferred in whispers for a moment.

"Madam, are you aware that falsifying ID is a crime?" the first guard asked.

Shad-Dari blinked in confusion. Her head was still throbbing. "Yes?"

"Listen, enh ... No one is going to prevent you from entering the city. That's not why we're here. We are only gathering information. So you don't have to tell stories." He offered her a placating smile. "Are you running from someone?"

Shad-Dari could only stare at him in mute astonishment. Was he joking? She couldn't tell.

"Everyone knows there is no such company as Sauú3," the second guard told her. "My friend, at least a better lie than this, please. You shame your ancestors with this nonsense. What even is a Sauúti-tongue Recovery Charter?"

The first guard chuckled. "Just tell the truth and there will be no harm done. Come. Your true occupation, please."

"I say we detain her." The second guard scowled at Shad-Dari. "She must be one of the Mahwéan maadiregi. You know those ones, always wandering beyond the boundary to do their experiments without applying for proper permits. Let her people come for her."

"What are you talking about?" Shad-Dari blurted out. "Mahwé is dead!" Her mind raced. What reason would there be to deny Sauú3, the biggest excavation company in the universe? And what was with the leather and shields? No one in Zezelam had carried a shield since—

"She is unwell," the first guard said, shaking his head at the second. He turned back toward Shad-Dari, speaking more slowly. "Whoever sold you this, it in nonsensical. Let us help you."

Her heart chilled in her chest. It was the strangest sensation, as though a shard of ice had gotten buried in her centre and was slowly claiming ground throughout her body. "Mahwé . . ." she rasped out.

"Ah, you see? Mad Mahwéan maadiregi," the second guard concluded, shaking his head. "Call the supervisor. I'm tired of these people breaking the rules all the time."

"Wait." Shad-Dari took a deep breath to steady her nerves. "This is the Mahwé-Zezépfeni Empire?"

"Empire?" The first guard laughed. "They have yet to conclude the terms of the alliance, and you call it an empire?"

The world spun for a moment as Shad-Dari realised the truth. The strange, old-fashioned uniforms. The primitive disinfection method. The fact that the guards had never heard of Sauú3. She had, somehow, gone back several hundred juzu.

Her mind reeled at the thought. No one she knew existed. Nothing she knew existed. The Empire was still in its formative juzu. There were no excavators, no Sauú3. Probably no Susu Nunyaa.

She backed away towards the door that led to the coast. Back to the only living things that could explain her predicament.

"What is she doing?"

"It looks like . . . Madam, we can help you!"

"Let me out," she whispered. Fear was climbing up her spine, but it was still just a vague threat, a sneaky shadow. She needed to be outside in the open air when the real terror struck. She needed sky and sand and clarity.

"Madam, just come and sit down, we will call your people to come—"

"Let me out!"

The guards balked at her frantic shriek, then rushed to open the door. Shad-Dari bolted into the open, gulping air as though she were drowning all over again.

How? How, how, how, how, how, how, how, how, how . . . The refrain propelled her forward, pumping through her muscles as she ran to the water, as she waded in, scanning the surface for a sign of the Mahu Mahadii. They had done this. Somehow, with their weird, wicked ways, their Mahu Mahadiiness. They were behind this unthinkable deviation, and they must fix it, they'd better fix it, or she would fling herself into the depths of the sacred sea and release what was left of her echo, oh, she would release every fragment of sound in her marrow, all her ugly, twisted, human flaws, corrupting the water forever.

"HOW?" she shouted, willing them to hear her, to come to her, to answer for what they had done. "WHYYYYYY?"

They didn't come, so she went deeper. She swam, and swam, and swam, stopping every so often to scream, praying—did she know how to pray? Was it the same as wishing?—that her voice would burrow into the water and lodge itself there like a thorn.

There. She saw them now, tentacles reaching up from beneath the surface to taste the air, taking the temperature of her sins. They must have decided that she was enough of a threat to merit their attention once again, because they were upon her seconds later, manhandling her, dragging her screaming back to the beach.

"How am I here? Now? How did you take me back in time?"

They didn't answer.

"Tell me, or I will defile Meshe-Shekhiiyem in ways you can't even dream of!"

They stopped just short of the coastline, holding her aloft as though they couldn't bear to have her touch the water. She could feel their consternation like a painful buzz under her skin.

"Time is not what you think it is," they said.

"What does that mean?"

"Time is not what you think it is."

The damned creatures and their cryptic ways! "Then what is it?"

"You cannot comprehend."

"Try me!"

"It does not begin and end. It does not stop or continue."

"But you can move through it? The way you move through space?"

There was a pause, and current zapped through her leg, as though the Mahu Mahadii were losing patience.

"We don't move through time. Time moves through us."

Shad-Dari's head was pounding too hard to make sense of that. "What does that mean? Why did it happen?"

"You were going to kill us. In the quiet, in the water, with your meddling. We had to stop you, to save ourselves."

Shad-Dari looked down at the swirling, smoke-like bodies. "I wasn't trying to kill anyone. I was trying to carry the sound fragments from below, the ones you left behind!"

"Your intentions are of no consequence. Your actions were a threat. The illicit fragments you threw into the water woke sounds from the bleakness. Sounds of the world that was and is no more. There is power in those sounds. That power does not fade and cannot be tempered. It carries time. It would destroy us all. You made matters worse by entering the water. It was necessary to remove you."

Dear Mother, they knew what she had done! They knew . . . but they had not turned her in. No, of course not. They wouldn't involve themselves in petty human affairs. They were not trying to punish her. Relieved, and then ashamed of herself for feeling relief, Shad-Dari pushed her confused emotions aside and tried to make sense of the creatures' explanation. Sounds from the world that was . . . They were talking about Mahwé. Was that what she had heard underwater? The screams of the dying? Was the robot she had seen in the water one of the Mahwé AIs, obliterated when the planet died?

"You could have just tossed me out of the lake," she pointed out.

"No. The sounds you woke wanted to be carried. They had . . . will. They were drawn to you, to your ability to wield them. If you had tried to do so, the results would have been cataclysmic. It was not enough to keep you from the water. It was necessary to remove you from their influence entirely. The only way was to take you into our bodies, which could act as a shield. We did not know that time had already begun to move through us."

Shad-Dari's head pounded as she absorbed their words. She didn't fully understand the Mahu Mahadii's magic, but she knew that they called up sound artefacts from below, one by one. It had never occurred to her—nor to the High Council, who would likely be furious if they knew—that there were sounds the creatures chose to leave undisturbed.

In the lake, they must have sensed the sounds from Mahwé's destruction and avoided them. But Shad-Dari's stolen fragments, pieces of the songs of the First Ones, had opened the door for those dangerous Mahwéan sounds. By diving into the water alone, she had provided the sounds with a vessel. The thought made her shiver with terror. Those time-twisted sounds would have ridden her to the surface, had the Mahu Mahadii not intervened.

She understood now that coming here, into the past, had been an accident. Shad-Dari could accept that, on one condition. "Fix it. Send me back. Forward. You know what I mean."

"We do not control time. It moves at will. Through us. Through you."

"No. No, you have to fix it!" Panic gripped her, making her

thrash in the Mahu Mahadii's grip. "I can't stay here! You have to fix it!"

They flung her onto the beach without further discussion and returned to the water. Shad-Dari scrambled to her feet, ran back to the water and leapt in. A host of tentacles rose up, grabbed her around the middle and pumped her full of electricity.

Her body was a starry sky, and then a supernova, and then a black, unfeeling void.

5.

WHEN SHE woke again, the first thing she was aware of was the gnawing ache in her belly. Food. Water. She could deal with the implications of being in the wrong time later—for now, old Zezelam would have to do. She would tell the guards that they were right, she was a liar. She was just a tourist from Ekwukwe, coming to see the sights, who'd bought an ID from a stranger. Harmless.

But when the gate swung open and she lurched inside, weak with hunger and fatigue, a different set of guards awaited her. This time they wore the uniform she knew, except it was darker in colour, sleeker, and topped with a helmet that revealed nothing of the wearer's face. She didn't step inside. She maintained her position, waiting to learn what time she had leapt into now. It was only when the guards spoke, their voices melodic and yet unmistakably other, that she realized they were not humans, but AIs, like the ones from Pinaa.

"Identify yourself," the guards repeated in unison.

Shad-Dari presented her ID once again. The robot guards listened, and then handed the device back to her.

"Implausible employment credential. The Sauú3 Company has been defunct for over seventy juzu. Bearing false witness is a crime. Therefore, by the authority of—"

Shad-Dari turned and fled.

She was no good at fishing or hunting, so she foraged and scavenged. On the second day, she found a dead crab on the beach. It took all her strength to crack its shell with a rock, but it sustained her for three more sunrises, until a bird snatched the remains from the embers of her dying fire and soared off to enjoy them.

Though the environment shifted, the things she gathered remained, as though by claiming them she had tied them to herself, freeing them from the vagaries of time.

Shad-Dari was a survivor. She always had been. She would make her way until she reached her own time. Only two things rattled her resolve—the phantom echoes, which had returned with a vengeance, and the environment. Just as she had learned which plants were poisonous, which insects to eat raw and which to cook first, everything would change. It could be one juzu later, or a thousand, five weeks earlier, or five centuries. She had no way of knowing.

Even in her sleep, now, the echoes clamoured for attention. She screamed herself awake to escape them. They greeted her beneath the pale sky and two suns. She counted the craters along the coast. Measured their circumferences. Guessed at when they had been made. She named the new plants that arose at one sunrise, only to be replaced at the next. She named them in honour of old gods and memories, the names of places on Ekwukwe that she had once thought to visit, or places on Órino-Rìn that she would find again.

All the while, the echoes lingered, chasing her, reaching for her with long, aged fingers.

That was the first week.

She was not moving. She understood now what the Mahu Mahadii had meant. She didn't seem to age forwards or backwards. She remained the same while the world—time—moved around her. Through her.

She thought of her crew. What had happened to them? Was Bed-Shek alive? Did they think Shad-Dari dead, drowned in the sisu'um lake? She missed their laughter and drunken jokes, their steady, reliable magic, their predictable behaviour. She missed Bed-Shek most of all.

She mapped the coastline, walking until she was certain she knew each landmark—the ones that would not change. The ridge of cliffs north of the boundary. The place where the sea ran through a hollow and rushed underground. The boundary itself, strong and certain in the face of change. If she ever reached a point where the boundary was no more—or not yet—she would know that time had gone too far. Back to the time of the First Ones, the time of the Seeding of the planet. Or ahead, to a time when humans no longer walked the world.

"I am not afraid," she murmured. If the First Ones came, she would greet them, and ask them questions, and hope they were as noble as history claimed. If humanity did not survive, she would mourn them, and carry on living until time shifted once more and they returned.

She was not afraid, she said, and yet it was hard to stop herself trembling, or jumping at the merest sound, or waking from sleep with her heart pounding hard enough to make her ears bleed.

She waded into the water to fish, and got somewhat better at it. She swam. If she ventured too far into the deep, or made too much noise, or caused too much chaos with her frenzied attempts to spear wriggling marine life, the Mahu Mahadii came to throw her back onto the beach. She asked them questions they could not be bothered to answer. Exhausted, she stopped asking.

That was the second week.

The echoes grew louder. Shad-Dari longed for sii'swaar to keep them at bay, but there was nothing here but the purest sounds of the natural world. Even the noises of human activity were out of reach, locked within the boundary. She shivered on sweltering nights and burned up on cold ones, her body a heaving, trembling mass of need.

"Go back," she told herself. Out loud, because the world was wrong without the voices of her crew, and the echoes jostled to fill up the silence. "Go to Zezelam. It doesn't matter whether time shifts. It doesn't matter. Go back and be human."

She walked to the boundary, paused near the gate, and then kept on walking. A changing environment was one thing. The changes beyond that wall were something else. To go to sleep in one room and wake up in another . . . To get to know people, only for them to cease to exist hours later . . . To start to build a life, only to watch it crumble . . . No, she was more human out here, alone. At least she knew who she was here. The sea never changed. The Mahu Mahadii never changed.

The echoes, too.

She no longer thought of return to her time. What would it give her but more pain? Shad-Dari was a survivor. Every time she thought of dying, she reminded herself that that was what the echoes wanted. And she decided to make them wait as long as she could.

She lost track of the weeks.

One morning she opened her eyes to find her eldest cousin Non'nofo standing over her.

Non'nofo swatted Shad-Dari's leg with a twig broom, leaving little scratches in the skin. "Are you still sleeping? Lazy girl—get up and go and fetch water. Do you have to be told?"

Shad-Dari felt as though her body had melted into the sand and her will wasn't strong enough to gather it up. A dream. Yes, it was a dream, and soon she would wake and it would be over.

"I said get up!"

Her cousin started to beat her harder, sending sand flying.

Shad-Dari felt nothing. Nothing. Nothing. And then—pain. Like a ship exploding inside her, tearing her ribs apart.

Shad-Dari burst out of her adult body and into her childhood one, off the beach at last, only to be plunged back into Tifaritu. Running through the caves on small, dusty legs, barefoot, glancing over her shoulder at the raised voices demanding to know where she had gone. Up, up, up.

And then she was on the beach again. Adult. Awake. Alone. Shaking so hard she feared she was having a fit. She dragged herself to the water and lay down, letting it wash over her, cool and refreshing. At least, awake, they could not find her.

"Sha'dar'dar? What are you doing?"

It was the voice of her sister. Little Kefi'ife. Shad-Dari kept her eyes closed. Still dreaming. Still dreaming. A small hand came to rest on her leg and shook it. No, still dreaming.

"Sha'dar'dar! Are you dead?" Followed by a sniffle, and then a plaintive wail. "Are you dead? Don't be dead, please!"

"Fool," Shad-Dari murmured. "You're the one who's dead."

The child laughed, relieved, and then lay down beside her sister. "What game are we playing? I don't know this one."

"Still dreaming." Shad-Dari had to say it aloud now, not just for her own benefit, but for the benefit of the ache in her chest. Her body appeared to have forgotten that these were old, ancient things, these memories, these people, these *feelings*, and Shad-Dari was all about progress.

She sat up and got to her feet. She saw the child out of the corner of her eye but refused to look in her direction. She wasn't real. No sense in validating a dream-spectre.

"Ooohhh! So much water! What place is this, Sha'dar'dar?"

"Stop calling me that. You're dead. Go away."

"Silly. I'm not dead! Are you going to swim?"

Shad-Dari ran into the water.

"Wait for me! Sha'dar'dar!" The child began to cry again.

Shad-Dari dove and swam, limbs slicing through the water. Once deep enough, she held her breath and plunged beneath the surface.

"Sha'dar'dar! Wait for me!"

Shad-Dari swam further. Deeper. Could a ghost echo drown? She experienced a momentary twinge of remorse—it seemed rather a cruel thing, to kill a child, even if it was a dream-spectre child. But then she reminded herself that the ghost was not supposed to be here, wandering around the timescapes of Zezépfeni, being a menace. She swam further. Deeper. Her lungs burned.

When the Mahu Mahadii came, she fought them. Thrashing, flailing, a tangle of limbs and tentacles. They won, of course. They flung her back. But when she landed in the wet sand, there was no little girl waiting for her.

Before long, the days began to blur together. The echoes, too. Sometimes it was Sha-sha-dar-dar-dar leading the procession of phantoms that trailed Shad-Dari along the coast. Other times it was No-no-no-no-no-no, for her cousin Non'nofo, or Ke-ke-kef-fi-fi-fi, for her baby sister Kefi'ife. Sometimes it was even

Esss-sssseeeee-essss-seeee, which made no sense, because her former girlfriend Essi'se was Órino-Rin born and bred, and had no echo.

Memories came unbidden and embodied, forcing her to relive them. Sneaking out of the caves, only to find that little Kefi had followed her. Annoyed at having to turn back rather than risk luring the child into harm's way and incurring the wrath of every adult that shared her blood. Waiting until Kefi had been given some chore to do, watching her scrunch up her little face in concentration, telling her how well she was doing—and then slipping away, ducking between two cousins and behind one sibling, and running as fast as her bare feet could go, heart soaring with each step.

Waking up in her hammock on the *Nuseh-Tor,* Essi'se at her side. Feeling the lateness of the hour in her marrow as her body wrenched itself out of sleep, contentment painting the day golden as second sunrise. Turning over to bury her face in Essi'se's back, adorning it with lazy kisses, waiting for the sleepy giggle that would rumble through both their bodies. Thinking it could last, this delicious thing that resembled joy, and fighting the creeping certainty that it would not.

Fafali's whisper-roar of a cheer when the Mahu Mahadii reported that the fragments they'd brought up from that brutal, lightless fissure at the very edge of the meridian came from the time of the Great Seeding. Shad-Dari almost passing out in Bed-Shek's arms, giddy with pride, wondering what this level of professional success could buy her. Standing before her supervisor and a representative of the High Council in Zezelam, being lauded for "outstanding service to human history," beaming as the leader of the Susu Nunyaa put a silver seal on her breast pocket.

Other memories, too. Bleaker ones. Stealing Im'mii's sii'swaar and playing it until she seized. Refusing to cry as he whipped her for her disobedience.

The rubble from the cave-in. The crushed, bloodied bodies dragged out of the wreckage. The piercing cries of her surviving aunt, and the way she would start keening halfway through some mundane task, and then stop, wipe her face and start on another task, leaving the first one incomplete. The recital of the names of the dead, required as part of the nightly prayer to ensure that their echoes reached Eh'wauizo. What had been the point of all those prayers? In this endless time, everyone was dead. Dead, yet refusing to die.

The world was all sand and sky and tiny little blades inside her, one for each ghost. Every time she inhaled, they slid a little deeper. She wouldn't cry, she decided, no matter how much they tried to hurt her. She had buried these people. She was done.

She heard the echoes laugh at her hubris.

Shad-Dari had not uttered any prayers or recited any names since leaving Ekwukwe. She had not allowed a single relative's name to leave her lips. Not one. Now, without warning, the names tumbled from her mouth, in order of age:

Hus'hu Mpepe
Ram'mari Mpepe
Thah'ahta Se'seruwa
Hle'hlenghi Se'seruwa
Lendi'le Se'seruwa

Ah'Bediah Se'seruwa
Ja'ja Se'seruwa
Kwa'kwamah Mpepe
Non'no'fo Mpepe
Amam'ma Tet'tet . . .

"Shad."

She looked up to see Essi'se's face, brow furrowed in familiar disappointment. She was in another memory. What had Shad-Dari done now? It was always something.

"You promised me you would stop."

Shad-Dari felt warm liquid trickle from her right ear and drop onto her bare shoulder. She reached up, dabbed at it. Looked at her finger. Blood. Why? Oh yes. She had gone to Mah Mmi'ino the night before for a little "mutilation."

Essi'se continued to gripe. Something about trust and sacrilege and self-destructive behaviour. And Shad-Dari lost her patience, because hearing all this the first time had been bad enough.

"What do you want from me? Why does everyone want something? All of you, so demanding, so greedy! If it's not Sauú3 and those self-righteous Susu Nunyaa, trying to swallow the entire universe—"

"Did I tell you to work for them?"

"What was I supposed to do? Waste away in those caves, waiting for them to collapse on me?"

"Shad . . ." A trace of remorse then, but it was too late.

"And you! Haven't I given you everything? Look at where you are! Isn't it enough?"

So Essi'se left, just as she had done in real time, if there was such a thing. And Shad-Dari tried to focus on fishing, but it was hard to do so with little Kefi sitting on the raft.

"What game are we playing?"

Shad-Dari ignored her. Memories were one thing—no point in fighting what had already happened—but hallucinations were something else. This was now. Or was it? In any case, Kefi had no business here. She had never been and would never be on Shad-Dari's raft, so Shad-Dari continued her recital.

"Hus'hu Mpepe, Ram'mari Mpepe, Thah'ata Se'seruwa . . ."

"What game are we playing?"

"Still dreaming. Still dreaming. Still dreaming."

"What game are we playing?"

"Silence! You're dead! Do you hear me? Dead!"

Shad-Dari made the mistake of turning to face the girl, a childish error that no true daughter of Tifaritu would make because they knew all about the ways monsters could entrap you. But Shad-Dari was Shad-Dari, a Tifaritu daughter no longer, and so she looked, and saw the bloodied, broken face of her youngest sibling stretch into a red, raw, crushed-jaw smile.

And she screamed loud enough to set the water frothing with Mahu Mahadii tentacles. She was still screaming as the creatures dragged her tragic little raft back to shore. Shad-Dari carried her sister's body from the raft, lay it down on the sand and keened, the way her aunt had, until the ghost faded away.

But she didn't cry. She had buried these people. She was done.

6.

BY THE time Shad-Dari sought out the Mahu Mahadii once more, every last one of her family's echoes had taken physical form. Ghastly amalgamations of the living versions of those she had lost and the battered corpses pulled from the rubble, they all followed her everywhere, everywhen, impervious to the vagaries of time that affected the rest of the world. Even Bed-Shek was among them, her body limp, her eyes closed, her waterlogged scales emitting sinister Aq'pa sounds that made Shad-Dari nauseous.

She couldn't sleep. She ate little and kept even less down, as though her own body was starting to decay in some sort of parasympathetic response to the walking dead. She staggered into the water, weak and gasping. She didn't have the energy to swim, so she treaded water. Waiting. Too tired to shout. Too tired to call out. Too tired to recite the names or chant "still dreaming" or make any attempt to chase the ghosts away.

This time, they followed her in and formed a ring around her. She wasn't sure whether they were trying to keep the Mahu Mahadii out or trying to keep her in. Maybe she should give in now, and die. Everyone died in the end. She had made her point. She had resisted. What was the point in fighting?

But the water came alive with electricity, tentacles writhing among swirling smoke. The Mahu Mahadii didn't expel her this time, not immediately. Perhaps she was too weak now to be a real threat. They did something else that was unusual—they spoke.

"You are tiresome," they said. "How can we be free of you?"

Ah. At last, the possibility of salvation. Shad-Dari grabbed it. "Free me of these phantom echoes and I will never trouble you again. I will seek permission before I enter the water, I will be as reverent as you like, I will stay in the shallows and know my place and honour Meshe-Shekhiiyem."

"We cannot free you. The echoes you speak of do not exist outside your mind."

Shad-Dari's arms sagged at the wearisome emptiness of their claim, and she struggled to stay above water now. "You sound like Mah Mmi'ino," she managed, her voice weak. "My mind might exaggerate them, but the echoes are here. They surround me as we speak. Don't you hear them?"

"Your own echo has faded beyond recognition. We hear nothing."

Fury shot through the numbness of her emotions. "I hear it loud and clear!"

"You imagine it. The entities that haunt you are neither echoes, nor ephemeral remains of your relatives. They are memories. Emotions."

Shad-Dari swallowed her fear. "No."

"The same sound-poison that killed your echo fed those so-called ghosts."

"No." She shook her head. She couldn't expect the Mahu

Mahadii to understand sii'swaar. "No, it sent them away. Every time I did it, they went quiet."

"Because they were feeding. After feeding, they came back stronger."

"No."

"That was why you had to fight them harder."

"No!"

And yet . . . Yes. She knew it was true. She had chosen not to know before, not to listen. She had chosen to run. Every day. Ever since *that* day. And now that she was too weak to run any further, it had caught up to her.

"Why didn't you tell me before?" she asked the Mahu Mahadii.

"You should have known. It is obvious."

To them, of course, everything was obvious. "Then why tell me now? I thought my feelings were of no consequence."

She sensed their impatience, a sudden jolt in the intensity of their energy. "You asked us to free you. We cannot free you from what is not. Only from what is. Your hunger causes you to engage in actions that are detrimental to us. Resolve it, so we may be spared the inconvenience of its existence."

"My . . . hunger . . ." They must think her so foolish, will-fully deaf to self-evident truths. She had always felt small in their presence, but this was the first time she felt ashamed. Her arms swept wider, now.

"That void you seek to fill cannot be filled. Cease trying. Accept what is."

She saw it now, clear as the water around her. *She* was the

Hunger, the ravenous monster that could not be named. She was Tlalala, insatiable, unrelenting.

Essi'se's parting words come back to her: "The problem isn't everyone else, Shad. The problem is you. That Aq'pa officer who mocked you the day you chose your name . . . He was wrong. You chose well. You knew in spirit, even then, exactly what you were. What you would become."

Shad-Dari. Insatiable Ghost. The name she had chosen, clueless as to its meaning, a butchered version of her own name, infused with the allure of another species. A name she had chosen out of fear that the void would engulf her, out of a desire for something more. She had thought she was choosing a new life. Saving herself. Instead, she had become the thing she feared.

It was said that Aq'pa names bound their bearers' souls, determined their fate. There would be no bartering with the gods once a name was given. It was sealed. Young Sha'dar'dar had found that fact curious and exciting, but harmless, a story with only one foot on solid ground. What did Aq'pa customs means to her, a human? Hers was a false name. The rules didn't apply.

Except, it seemed, they did.

Bed-Shek should have told her . . . Ah. Bed-Shek *had* told her, and often. Told her to be wiser, more responsible. Made her swear on her echo. And Shad-Dari had done what she always did. She had broken her promise.

What had she been, if not insatiable? Starved for escape, for relief, consuming sii'swaar to feed the void inside her. What was she, if not a ghost? Wandering the worlds, pretending to live, knowing deep down that she had died in the caves with her family?

The echoes swirled, their whispers persistent. Loudest of all, her own. *Sha-sha-sha-dar-dar* . . . And at last she understood why they were so loud, so present, why the air of Órino-Rin had not dented them in the slightest. They came from within. She had birthed them in a dark and hollow place. They were not her siblings or her parents. They were her children.

The Mahu Mahadii sank below the waves. The echoes drew closer, forming a wall around her, as they had done when they were living. Hemming her in, making her claustrophobic. Shielding her from the harsh realities of the world, from loneliness, from solitude. A prison, but a fortress, too.

She had wanted so desperately to be free of all those bodies taking up space and air in the caves. All those clamouring voices. And then, one day, her wish had been granted. They were gone, taking all she knew, all she was, with them. Twenty-nine chunks of Sha'dar'dar, gouged out and flung away without warning, when she was too young to grasp what it meant to only be part of a person.

The echoes dropped to gentle, soothing whispers, lifting her out of the water, leading her back to the shore. She realized then that she had buried all the people she had lost, but one. Sha'dar'dar was dead, too, echo and all. The child deserved a funeral, so Shad-Dari stood at the water's edge and said the words of farewell, and then recited all the names of the deceased—all thirty of them. She didn't add Bed-Shek's. She hoped the Aq'pa was still alive.

The echoes heaved a single sigh of relief. That was all they had wanted. To be heard. To be honoured. She felt them leave her, like the vestiges of sleep fading in the face of a new dawn.

She saw them rise, up, up, up, into the stars that had once called to her. Home to Eh'wauizo, at long last.

For the first time since childhood, Shad-Dari broke down and cried.

7.

THE QUIET was devastating.

How strange that she had sought it out before, longed for it, broke contracts and rules and promises to find it. There were no echoes anymore, here in the world where time passed through her. She had willed them gone and they had left her. In life, in the past. In spirit, in the present. And now she was alone, as she had always and never wanted to be.

Shad-Dari slept. When she was not sleeping she wished she were, because at least in her dreams she could travel, be elsewhere, elsewhen, and feel other things. Each time she woke and remembered, she greeted the grief anew. She was a hungry ghost shot through with holes, too broken to live, yet too craven to die. Or was it the other way around?

She only got up when her body's needs spoke too loudly to be ignored, but she returned to sleep soon afterwards, in the little shelter she had found for herself. A mockery of a cave, really, a hollow in a fallen meteor. A space so shallow it would earn the scorn of any Ekwukwe home. But it was warm and dry and shielded her from the elements, and even though it was a hole in a fallen rock from the skies and not a true cave, it reminded her of home.

And then, one day, when she had fallen asleep outside, she

woke to find that the light of the two suns danced just so on the water, and it was beautiful. She sat up and watched it for a time. She realized, in great surprise, that it brought her . . . not joy. No, not that. Pleasure, perhaps? Solace? She wasn't sure. She only knew that she experienced, for those few moments, something other than despair.

The next time she went out to fish, she sought permission, as she had promised the Mahu Mahadii she would.

"Meshe-Shekhiiyem, Great Spirit of the Deep, I seek your leave to enter your waters in search of sustenance. Grant me life, as I grant you honour."

She waited, but of course the great Meshe-Shekhiiyem didn't deign to respond.

Well, if she drowned she would know that her prayers were not accepted.

She didn't drown.

Over the months that followed, Shad-Dari turned her little raft into a proper boat, held together with twine and gum and waterproofed with paint made from meteor dust and the fat of the rodents she had managed to hunt. She began to relish not knowing what the day had in store, or what type of world she would find when she stepped out of her hollow.

She learned to tell medicine from poison, or how to use one to make the other, for they were often kindred. She learned to take educated guesses at the properties of new plants, to recognize that while the Mother made different faces for her children, the structure underneath was the same. She learned to set traps that killed quickly, for dying was painful, though death was release.

She learned to listen to the silence. And she learned that it was rarely silent at all. All the time she had spent focused on the sounds in her head had deprived her of the sounds in the world. She heard them now. They spoke to her and brought her news.

Ships flying overhead—their drones too low to be excavator ships, so they must be passenger ships or cargo ships. Birdsong, but higher-pitched than the day before—a portent of bad weather.

Every once in a while, though, she would hear actual silence. Sounds sucked from the world, as though her ears had been blocked. Always brief. Always disconcerting.

After some time, Shad-Dari stopped asking for permission to enter the sea. Instead, she spoke to Meshe-Shekhiiyem as she would an old friend.

"Greetings, Sea. Are you going to be generous today, or should I just trek through the forest? I'd rather not, if I'm honest. I don't know whether those giant stinging things are still around, and I could use a break from their venom."

On the few occasions she tried to enter Zezelam out of sheer curiosity, the guards took one look at her and dismissed her as one of the outcasts who lived in exile outside the boundary—voluntarily or otherwise—and were forbidden from re-entry. She made peace with her fate. There was nothing left for her in the city, anyway. Even if Sauú3 existed, its headquarters still on the pristine hills of Kwartey Island beyond that boundary wall, it made no difference now. Her old life was gone. There was no way back to her ship. Her crew. Her friends.

Shad-Dari carved out a new life for herself that looked nothing like the one she had envisioned. There was no up, up, up anymore. No goals. No glory. No wealth. No Ducha'ga syhh'ras. There was sky and sea and sand. There was coast and cave, and inland sometimes there was forest, other times desert. Shad-Dari found that none of these things inflamed her passions, for better or worse. She wasn't even sure she still had any passions. She thought of her dead family and lost friends often, with sadness and some regret, but despair seemed to have tired of her company. She was sometimes weary, and sometimes pleased. Sometimes annoyed, never angry. Sometimes curious, never obsessive.

She pondered this new state of affairs regularly. She often imagined Bed-Shek scowling at her in characteristic impatience, signing, *Fool. It's called contentment.*

The thought always made her smile.

Many juzu passed. Decades. At least, it must have been decades, but Shad-Dari had no way to tell for certain. She felt no older, yet her hair had grown long, and when she studied the twisted ends she found them shot through with grey. Her body was still strong, but not as it had been in her heyday. She wondered whether she could still carry sound fragments. Apart from the occasional act of self-defence against some natural threat, she'd had little cause to use sound magic here.

At times, she heard the drone of an excavator ship, being not far from the Zezelam spaceport. She didn't often come to this side of the boundary, though it was good for fishing—the water was deep, but too close to the Mahu Mahadii birthing grounds. Now that the creatures no longer thought her a menace, she had no desire to irk them. She had come on foot instead, and was picking through the detritus of an old outcast settlement in search of scraps she could use, when the ship approached.

She wouldn't have bothered to look up this time if she hadn't recognized the ship's signature. Even now, after all this time, it was locked into her soul like an echo. The *Nuseh-Tor*. She would recognize it anywhere, in any time. Her heart jumped. Her ship. Her crew?

She ran. It was silly, childish, even, but she couldn't help herself. She had to see it land at the edge of the water to release its Mahu Mahadii passengers before the crew took their haul to the Susu Nunyaa. She had to know whether her crew were alive, in whatever time this was.

Shad-Dari reached the port and hid in a crater beside the boundary, peering at the array of ships. There, the one nearest the water. The *Nuseh-Tor* was as beautiful as ever, as in good repair as when she'd been on it. She smiled as the secondary ramp came down, and then seven Mahu Mahadii drifted along it and into the water. She shifted position so she could watch the crew emerge from the other side, as the secondary ramp slid back into place. She saw the main ramp come down, but she was in the wrong position to see the crew's faces, so she took a risk.

Climbing out of the crater, she walked along the boundary and stood right at the edge of the port. In full view.

Just a quick look, she told herself. The first figure to emerge was an Aq'pa. Her pulse quickened. Not just any Aq'pa. Bed-Shek. It was all she could do not to shout to her friend. She had to control herself. What good would it do? They must think her long dead.

Kga'arah was next, and then Rori'iro. Shad-Dari blinked, confused. The boy still looked like the gangly youth she remembered, yet to grow into his body. He still bore that ridiculous kartel tattoo on his neck. And then she saw the captain, and understanding dawned. Those were her own legs, striding across the floor. Her own features forming a triumphant smirk. Her own gaze, lifting to the observation deck above . . .

And Shad-Dari looked up too, remembering. She saw the two Susu Nunyaa initiates, faces pressed against the window. She winked, just as she had done all those juzu ago, when she had occupied the body on the ground. The initiates giggled. Young Shad-Dari grinned, basking in the adoration, and the crew passed through the open boundary gates and into the holy city.

Old Shad-Dari couldn't move. Had she really just seen her younger self? She remembered that event so clearly—the delivery of the sound fragments that would have catapulted her to stardom, had she lingered in that world long enough. She knew what would happen next. The handover, to four awestruck, gushing Susu Nunyaa, who would insist on opening the drums that very evening to confirm that they indeed contained the songs of the First Ones. The presentation of the SeKarah's seal, the highest commendation an excavation crew could receive from the Susu Nunyaa leader. Cheers and adulation.

And then she and her crew would sail back to Órino-Rin, make their report, and dock the *Nuseh-Tor* safely at the Ducha'ga depot before heading to Shad-Dari's shack to celebrate. They would head out the very next morning for their next dig. Not even a moment to breathe. Always on to the next thing. Up, up, up.

She stood there, staring at the ship. The very same ship, her mark all over it. It was hers, still. She could go down there and open it and walk around inside, as if no time had passed. Well, no, she couldn't. She was an outcast. If she made any move to enter the port, guards would be upon her in minutes.

You've been here before. Remember?

How could she ever forget? And yet she couldn't tear herself away. An hour passed. Another. She was still standing there when the crew emerged, returning to the ship without their drums. Fresh ones would be waiting at the dock in Ducha'ga.

Shad-Dari stared at her crew, her friends. Tears streamed down her face as she wished them a silent farewell. And when she turned her attention to her younger self, her breath caught in her throat. Young Shad-Dari was looking right at her, an expression of mild curiosity on her face.

And Shad-Dari remembered now. She was the woman she had locked eyes with on that trip, who had so unsettled her for reasons she couldn't explain then. Perhaps she had known, on some instinctive level, that the older woman had no business being there.

She remembered something else, too. The stolen sound

fragments that had caused all the trouble were in Young Shad-Dari's pocket at that very moment. If she could get them, if she could warn herself, the catastrophe at the sisu'um would never happen. Except it had already happened. Hadn't it? Could it be undone? Or would she only cause further disruption by interfering?

For Young Shad-Dari, these would have been vital questions with practical implications. She would already be down there, consequences be damned. But Old Shad-Dari was, well, older. Wiser, perhaps. The past was past. It had taken her long enough to accept that. And in truth, she would change nothing. The series of events that led her here had set her free. If she had not tried to dispose of those stolen fragments, she would have remained an insatiable ghost.

The two versions of her held each other's gazes for what might have been aeons or seconds, and then Young Shad-Dari looked away, distracted by something Rori'iro had said. The crew boarded the ship. The secondary ramp opened up once more, and the Mahu Mahadii rose up out of the water and into the ship. Different individuals from the ones that had made the last trip, but that was a distinction that hardly mattered.

Except it mattered to Shad-Dari. One of those seven would swallow her whole and then vomit her up in the sacred sea. Saving her. Saving everyone.

She watched the ramp close, and then the *Nuseh-Tor* sailed away to meet its fate.

❋

A few days later, Shad-Dari found a body in the water while she was fishing. The body floated along the surface, buffeted by the waves. Clothes of brown bark cloth. Simple work boots. A pilgrim. Shad-Dari had seen enough of them leaving for or returning from their superstitious trek to the deep.

She had always thought them fools. Armed with nothing but their wits, determined to prove themselves worthy of a life of gilded, gloried service by flinging themselves into the sea and not drowning. Nonsense, all of it. As if Meshe-Shekhiiyem could be bothered with the dreams of Susu Nunyaa initiates. As if anyone cared whether a few of them never made it home. There were more than enough of them as it was, floating through the world, supposedly knowing best.

At least, that was what Young Shad-Dari would have thought. The one who cared more than she let on. The one who resented her masters enough to rob them, but not enough to leave them. This Shad-Dari had no such concerns. She looked at the limp body bobbing in the water and thought only of whether it would be worth the effort to bring it in.

Time could shift in the process. Surely it must soon, as it had not yet shifted from the day she saw herself. She might carry the person all the way to shore, only to find that they were already beyond help. They might vanish moments later, dead and gone, forgotten, or still forming in their mother's womb. What was the point? She might as well leave them for the serpents, who deserved a good meal as much as she did.

And yet Shad-Dari found herself steering the boat closer, and closer, and reaching out to grab a pair of waterlogged legs, and realizing she would need to get into the water. So she did.

She jumped in and took hold of the body, and heaved until she had gotten it into the boat, then climbed in beside it.

Her heart leapt, and then sank. The pilgrim had Kefi'ife's face. Or perhaps the face Kefi would have had, if she had lived to her late teens. Shad-Dari bent to listen for breath. There it was—faint. So the pilgrim lived. For now.

And even though she knew it was pointless, Shad-Dari ferried the pilgrim to shore, took her into the hollow and nursed her back to health. She learned, when the young woman woke, that her name was Ruah-Mmaru.

Time didn't shift. Each day Shad-Dari woke, the pilgrim was still there. It would happen soon, Shad-Dari told herself. It was inevitable.

And yet, it didn't happen. Time moved as it had done before, as though it had grown tired of its wild adventure and was eager to go home.

Shad-Dari felt relieved, yet also a little unnerved. What would life be, if there were no more time shifts?

Ruah-Mmaru was strange, in the way that all Susu Nunyaa were. Wound tight as hair spirals, saying more with their tone and manner than with their words. She was polite, of course, and grateful, but the tension in her neck spoke of disdain. She resented having to rely on an outcast, yet thought herself entitled to Shad-Dari's assistance.

"Don't you have any melon?" she would ask, wrinkling her

nose and picking at the unfamiliar meat Shad-Dari offered. "I have a delicate stomach."

When she forgot herself, haughtiness reared its head. "You wouldn't understand," she'd say. "It's not your fault—you're a heathen outcast. If I had some recordings with me, I could teach you . . ."

And Shad-Dari, who no longer knew how to take offense, only laughed.

How odd, she thought, to be so contrary, and so unaware of it. What a needlessly complex way to live. To think she had once lived in a similar fashion.

Yet she enjoyed the initiate's company. True, Shad-Dari could hardly be picky—she hadn't spoken to another human being in ages—but she admired Ruah-Mmaru's genuine desire to serve and was amused by her Susu Nunyaa ways.

They spoke of many things. The harsh climate and the sacred sea, the mysterious Mahu Mahadii. Though Shad-Dari thought of her crew, grateful that she had been granted the chance to see them again, she couldn't share her true experiences with the initiate. Instead, she spoke vaguely of seeing old friends enter the city and coming to terms with the fact that she would never see them again. She spoke of letting go, something that came easier to her now. Something she had come to embrace. She spoke of living fully in the present. Ruah-Mmaru squirmed as though the concept were blasphemous.

Mainly, they spoke of Ruah-Mmaru's crisis of faith. The delivery of the fragments from the Great Seeding, the fragments Shad-Dari's crew had found, had set the Susu Nunyaa aflame. The fragments spoke of a history drastically different from the one the Susu Nunyaa knew and proclaimed. The fragments implied that Zezépfeni was not the planet of the First Ones, firstborn of the five and rightful leader of the system. Shad-Dari had no investment in such political squabbles, but Ruah-Mmaru was at a crossroads. She didn't know whether to proceed with her vows and bind herself to the order, or turn her back on everything she had worked for.

"Why did you save my life?" Ruah-Mmaru asked one evening, as they sat eating the food Shad-Dari had foraged earlier. "I know outcasts don't care for us."

"Is that what they teach you in the Temple?"

"We don't need to be taught. If the Susu Nunyaa advocate for someone to be exiled, it's only natural that those exiled will resent us. If people choose exile, it's because they see no value in being in the holy city, and so, again, it's only natural that they resent us."

Shad-Dari smiled. "So in all the world, there are only those who admire you and those who despise you? What of those who are indifferent?"

The pilgrim frowned, apparently annoyed by the question. "No one is indifferent."

"I see." Shad-Dari licked her fingers. She had discovered, in recent juzu, that there was nothing quite as delectable as a perfectly ripe fruit. "I don't know why I saved you, to be honest. I just did. When I saw your face, it reminded me of my sister, Kefi."

"I resemble her?"

"Not at all. You did, in that moment. Maybe Meshe-

Shekhiiyem made me see Kefi's face, so I wouldn't be tempted to throw you back into the water."

Ruah-Mmaru was quiet for some time, her expression flickering and shifting, as though uncertain what it wanted to portray. And then she said, with a drawn-out exhalation, "I dislike you very much."

Shad-Dari laughed. "That's the most honest thing you have said to me! Well done."

"No! It's not right to dislike another. Love and compassion for all is integral to a life of service."

Shad-Dari heard the anxious longing behind the words, the desperate desire to be what one was not, and recognized it. "You feel what you feel," Shad-Dari told her. "Pretending to feel otherwise serves no one."

Again, the pilgrim was quiet for a while. "Is it possible to find truth within a lie?"

"Yes. And to find lies within the truth. The world is not so simple as we might like it to be."

"No. I suppose it isn't."

"You will be fine."

Ruah-Mmaru looked up. "I know. My injuries aren't so serious."

"I'm not talking about your injuries. Whether you decide to leave the Susu Nunyaa or stay, you will be fine."

"How is that possible?"

"You want to serve your people, yes? So serve them. Only you can decide the best way to do so. Even within the Susu Nunyaa, there is good work to be done. Maybe that is the work for you."

It would be a stretch to say that she grew to love the girl over the eight days they spent together, but she felt grateful to her and wished her well. She saw in the initiate a sliver of the hunger she had carried herself for so long, and the potential to wear it better than Shad-Dari had.

"You saved her."

"What?" Shad-Dari looked up from putting on her boots.

Ruah-Mmaru stood up. She was healed now, and ready to return to her people. "Your sister. Kefi. You couldn't save her in the caves when you were a child. But you saved me, and I had her face, even if it was only for a moment. It was a message from Meshe-Shekhiiyem. From the Mother. A message letting you know that by saving me, you redeemed yourself. You saved Kefi."

These words left Shad-Dari feeling warm inside, though she didn't believe them. It was the sort of convoluted reasoning one would expect from Susu Nunyaa. But she gave the pilgrim a grateful smile and said, "It's time to go home."

She took Ruah-Mmaru to the gate near the spaceport, bid her farewell, and then took the boat out beyond the Mahu Mahadii birthing grounds and lay inside, looking up at the stars. The sky was a pale purple, as pretty as it had ever been, the world quiet, free from echoes.

Shad-Dari closed her eyes and slept. She never woke. After a time, Meshe-Shekhiiyem swallowed her body like an offering, echo and all.

❁

The afterlife was a Ducha'ga syhh'ra—relatives gossiping, siblings screaming, mad Mahwéan maadiregi muttering mantras, blue-red mutant crabs in rapid-fire clicking conversation with robots, Mahu Mahadii waving their tentacles in a manner reminiscent of dancing. There was Im'mii, marketing sii'swaar to laughing Sauú3 recruits who reminded him that no sound was illicit here. There were even Ts'jenene raevaagi, swapping sacred sonic histories.

The syhh'ra to end all syhh'ras. Clearly, Shad-Dari had made it.

You've been here before. Remember?

Yes. In other lives, other bodies. Yes, yes. This was where everything began/ended/began again. Was she inside the Mother or was the Mother inside her? Was there a difference? Did it matter? Probably not. At least, not anymore. Shad-Dari laughed and went to join the dancing.

Dying was painful. Living, too. But letting go was release.

Acknowledgements

It takes a village to write a book. This is my village, aka The Sauútiverse Collective: Eugen Bacon, Xan van Rooyen, Jude Umeh, Wole Talabi, Stephen Embleton, Akintoba Kalejaye, Adelehin Ijasan, Ikechukwu Nwaogu, Dare Segun Falowo and of course Fabrice Guerrier, who showed us how the whole collaborative worldbuilding thing could work. I am beyond grateful to my Sauúti family for all the thrilling brainstorming sessions, the time spent reading and reviewing each other's work, and all your feedback on *Songs*. Thank you. You are the reason this book exists, especially because you believed in it even when I didn't. Being part of this incredible group of creators is the highlight of my writing career.

Wole, thank you for writing the foreword and encouraging me to just "do the thing" when I feared I'd never finish the story. As the one who brought us all together, I kind of think of you as our Captain - in an egalitarian Sauútiverse way, of course. ☺

Toba and Stephen, a million thanks for capturing the essence of Shad-Dari's story so beautifully in the artwork. I'm still blown away by how well your distinct styles come together to create the perfect piece! There are no words for how much

I love the art you've both created for this book, and for the Sauútiverse in general. We should start talking about the cover for my next novel . . .

Gregory A. Wilson, thank you for hosting the cover reveal event and for your infectious enthusiasm. It was a pleasure to cyber-meet you.

Emily Bell, editor/publisher extraordinaire, you are a gem. Thank you for your empathy, for loving this story as much as I do, championing it from the get-go, seeing all the things I missed and honoring both my voice and the Sauútiverse spirit at every turn. Thank you to Chris Bell for taking such care with the book interior and facilitating the contracts, Core Hartley and AJ Super for helping the engine run smoothly and Tessa Anouska for proofreading the novella. Atthis Arts is a prime example of why indie publishers are so precious and vital. Akpe, medaase, ke a leboga—thank you in all the languages of my soul.

Thank you to Bieke van Aggelen of the African Literary Agency; even though this work predates our partnership, your support and encouragement has been a gift.

Tlotlo Tsamaase, Gothataone Moeng and Joyce Chng, thank you for writing such glorious blurbs. Tlotlo, I will forever appreciate your years-long investment in me and my work. Gothataone, it means so much that you read this even though it's not quite your cup of Five Roses! Barolong Seboni, thank you for reading it as well. #Petlo for life! Thank you to Doug Cosper and Stewart C Baker for your time, careful consideration and insight, which helped whip the book into shape. I appreciate you tremendously.

Thank you to my beloved sangha and my fellow writers and artists, working hard to give meaning to this baffling thing called life, and my family (blood and chosen) for your unconditional love and support.

Finally, because it was the devastation of losing you that shaped Shad-Dari's journey:

The late, great K-Bed, the one who always asked, "But are you happy?" and told me my only job was to fly. Please don't be annoyed that I call you K-Bed. It's the name you scrawled into every book you ever bought, so of course I always called you that in my heart. You took countless universes with you when you went. I hope you're proud of the new ones I'm crafting.

And BCJ . . . I haven't forgotten your prediction. Let's see if you were right about that the way you were about so many other things. I think I struggled so much with Shad-Dari because I knew she had come to show me how to let you go, and it took me a while to be ready. I'm growing my life now, like you told me to.

The only way out is through. I love you both from the depths of my echo.

CHERYL S. NTUMY is a Ghanaian writer of short fiction and novels of speculative fiction, young adult fiction and romance. Her work has appeared in *FIYAH Literary Magazine; Apex Magazine; World Literature Today; Best of World SF Vol. 3* and *Year's Best African Speculative Fiction 2022*, among others. Her work has also been shortlisted for the Nommo Award for African Speculative Fiction, the Commonwealth Writers Short Story Prize and the Miles Morland Foundation Scholarship. She is part of the Saúuti Collective, which created a shared universe for Afrocentric speculative fiction, and a member of Petlo Literary Arts, an organization that develops and promotes creative writing in Botswana.

WOLE TALABI is an engineer, writer, and editor from Nigeria. He is the author of the critically acclaimed novel *Shigidi And The Brass Head Of Obalufon* which was named one of the best fantasy books of 2023 by *The Washington Post*. His fiction has appeared in speculative fiction magazines and anthologies globally and has been translated into 7 languages. He has been a finalist for several major awards including the Hugo, Nebula and Locus awards, the Caine Prize for African Writing and the Nommo Award, which he won in 2018, 2020, and 2024. In 2022 he won the Sidewise Award for Alternate History for "A Dream of Electric Mothers". He has edited three anthologies including *Africanfuturism* and *Mothersound: The Saúutiverse Anthology*. His debut collection of stories, *Incomplete Solutions,* was published in 2019 by Luna Press, followed by the collection *Convergence Problems*, published in 2024 by DAW Books. He likes scuba diving, elegant equations and oddly shaped things. He currently lives and works in Australia.

Milton Keynes UK
Ingram Content Group UK Ltd.
UKHW030517301024
450418UK00001B/12